MILLER FAMILY WRAP-UP STORY

MILLER FAMILY ROMANCES

NATALIE DEAN

DEDICATION

I'd like to dedicate this book to YOU! All of my wonderful readers that have been following my stories over the years.

Thank you to my biggest fans.... There's a lot of you! Jess, Bernie, Wren, Judy, Sherry, Vicci, Phyllis, Debbie, Indra, Jennifer, Carol, Jeanette, Margaret, Paul, and I know there's more I didn't list. But thank you all!

And I can't leave out my wonderful mother, son, sister, and Auntie. I love you all, and thank you for helping me make this happen.

Most of all, I thank God for blessing me on this endeavor.

AND... I've got a special team of advance readers who are always so

helpful in pointing out any last minute corrections that need to be made. I'm so thankful to those of you who are so helpful!

OTHER BOOKS BY NATALIE DEAN

Miller Family Saga

BROTHERS OF MILLER RANCH

Miller Family Saga Series 1

Her Second Chance Cowboy

Saving Her Cowboy

Her Rival Cowboy

Her Fake-Fiance Cowboy Protector

Taming Her Cowboy Billionaire

Brothers of Miller Ranch Complete Collection

MILLER BROTHERS OF TEXAS

Miller Family Saga Series 2

The New Cowboy at Miller Ranch Prologue

Humbling Her Cowboy

In Debt to the Cowboy

The Cowboy Falls for the Veterinarian

Almost Fired by the Cowboy

Faking a Date with Her Cowboy Boss

Miller Brothers of Texas Complete Collection

BRIDES OF MILLER RANCH, N.M.

Miller Family Saga Series 3

Cowgirl Fallin' for the Single Dad

Cowgirl Fallin' for the Ranch Hand

Cowgirl Fallin' for the Neighbor

Cowgirl Fallin' for the Miller Brother

Cowgirl Fallin' for Her Best Friend's Brother

Cowboy Fallin' in Love Again

Brides of Miller Ranch Complete Collection

Miller Family Wrap-up Story

(An update on all your favorite characters!)

~

Copper Creek Romances

BAKER BROTHERS OF COPPER CREEK

Copper Creek Romances Series I

Cowboys & Protective Ways

Cowboys & Crushes

Cowboys & Christmas Kisses

Cowboys & Broken Hearts

Cowboys & Second Chances

Cowboys & Wedding Woes

Cowboys' Mom Finds Love

Baker Brothers of Copper Creek Complete Collection

CALLAHANS OF COPPER CREEK

Copper Creek Romances Series 2

Making a Cowgirl

Marrying a Cowgirl

Christmas with a Cowgirl

Trusting a Cowgirl

Dating a Cowgirl

Catching a Cowgirl

Loving a Cowgirl

Marrying a Cowboy

Callahans of Copper Creek Complete Collection

KEAGANS OF COPPER CREEK

Copper Creek Romances Series 3

Some Cowboys are Off-Limits

Some Cowgirls Love Single Dads

Some Cowboys are Infuriating

Some Cowboys Don't Like City Girls

Some Cowboys Heal Broken Hearts

Some Cowgirls are Worth Protecting

Some Cowboys are Just Friends (Coming August 2024)

Though I try to keep this list updated in each book, you may also visit my website nataliedeanauthor.com for the most up to date information on my book list.

CONTENTS

PART III
BRIDES OF MILLER RANCH, N.M.
WRAP-UP

MILLER FAMILY WRAP-UP STORY DESCRIPTION

Okay readers... if you haven't read all of the Miller Family stories, you may not want to read this wrap-up story until you do.

This wrap-up story is really for all of you who loved reading about the Millers and want to know more! It essentially gives a 'Where are they now?" update.

As of January 2022, the Miller Family series has a total of seventeen sweet love stories! It can get confusing with so many couples so I'm laying it out here which couples were in which series, listed in order of when I wrote them.

Brothers of Miller Ranch - Montana (First Miller Family Series)
- Benedict (Ben) and Chastity
- Bart and Missy
- Bradley and Sophia
- Benji and Danielle (Dani)
- Bryant and Keiko

Miller Brothers of Texas (Second Miller Family Series)
- •. Samuel and Virginia (Ginny) (Found in Prologue)
- Solomon and Frenchie
- Silas and Theodora (Teddy)
- Sterling and Elizabeth
- Salvatore (Sal) and Nova
- Simon and Leilani

Brides of Miller Ranch, N.M. New Mexico (Third Miller Family Series)
- Charity and Alejandro (and Savannah)
- Cassidy and Mick
- Clara and Nathan
- Charlie and Daisy
- Cici and Baz
- Papa (Montgomery) and Jeanette

PART I

BROTHERS OF MILLER RANCH WRAP-UP

1

Benedict

*B*en wiped his hands on his jeans, standing there on the sidewalk, looking up at the building that seemed like it was looming over them.

"Are you okay, Daddy?"

Ben looked down to his boy, who let go of Chastity to grab Ben's hand instead. He looked so much like his mother, with her dark eyes and thick lashes, but every now and then, Ben could see some of his features in the little guy too.

It was hard to believe that Danny was almost five, and he was about to head into his very first day of kindergarten. Hadn't he just been born the year before? Hadn't he just started speaking last week? And yet, it was definitely a school-aged kid standing in front of him, decked out with a superhero backpack and sneakers.

"I'm fine, Danny. Just excited for your first day. You're gonna have so much fun."

Danny narrowed his eyes and *goodness*, he was definitely the spitting image of his mother. "Are you sure? What if I don't make friends?"

"You will, buddy."

"You're gonna have a great first day," Chastity piped in.

"Okay. I hope so."

"Give mommy one more kiss before you go," she added.

"Moooom, everyone is gonna see."

"Everyone else is getting kisses from their mommies, daddies or guardians. You'll fit right in."

"...I dun think that's right."

"Please?"

"...alright. But if I get made fun of, you owe me."

Ben had no idea where he'd learned that, and he also had no idea what they could possibly "owe" their child other than a happy meal, but those were things that could be talked about after his first day.

"Deal," Chastity said, offering their little tyke a hand. He shook it, then stood on tiptoe while she bent towards him. Danny placed a quick kiss on her cheek, then looked around furtively. Perhaps unsurprisingly, no one flooded out of the school to mock him.

"Now it's my turn."

"*Daaaaaddddd!*"

"Come on, it can't be so embarrassing to give your dad a kiss."

"I guess."

Despite Danny's suspicious look, he did indeed plant one on Ben's cheek before letting out one of those impatient sounds that only kids could make.

"Can I go now?"

"Alright, Danny, go ahead."

"Okay, I love you. I'll see you later!"

At that, he rushed away as fast as his legs would carry him. Ben reached out for Chastity, and she gripped his hand tightly.

"When did he grow up so much?" Ben asked, trying not to sound mournful and failing pretty spectacularly.

"I don't know. But I'm gonna lose it when Dakota and Daniella start school."

"Thankfully we've got a couple of years before that."

"The time goes so fast though."

"That it does." Ben squeezed her hand and turned to her, pulling her in close. "But I'm glad to spend that time with you."

"Awww, you really know how to talk to a girl, don't cha?"

"No, but I might have an idea of how to talk to the love of my life."

Chastity blushed beautifully, the red rising up her neck and over her cheeks. After all their years together, Ben had never gotten tired of that blush.

"You're being real smooth for an emotionally devastating day."

"Hah, I don't know about emotionally devastating, but I might still be in denial."

"That's alright. Want to go be in denial over a plate of biscuits and gravy?"

"I knew there was a reason I love you."

She squeezed his hand again. "I love you too, darling."

Ben tilted his head down to give her a kiss, and she returned it, sweet and kind and perfect, as always.

"So, about those biscuits and gravy?"

He couldn't help but laugh at that. "You're on."

But he still held her hand the entire way to the car and the drive back home.

2

Chastity

"kay, that take was good, but can we do a safety one just to be sure?"

"Of course," Chastity said with a grin. She was in LA on a filming shoot, and at that moment she was exhausted through and through, but it was better to suck it up for another fifteen minutes than to have to come in for reshoots another day.

"Perfect. Let's run it from your entrance."

Chastity nodded and went to her mark. Most of her work in the past two years had been educational, which meant there wasn't a ton of blocking and a whole lot more sitting. But when she'd been invited to do a series of sketches for a popular internet news channel, she'd jumped on it.

She just hadn't counted on her segments being so popular that they invited her back again and were filming enough sketches to use for three of their episodes in the future. Normally that would never work for a news channel—as it needed to be current by its own nature—but their format with pre-filmed comedy breaks was perfect for stocking up on footage.

"Action!"

With one last deep breath, Chastity went through the take again. Thankfully, it went just as well as the previous one and their safety was in the bag. And thank goodness, because Chastity's feet were killing her. Next time she wouldn't wear new shoes!

Still, she said her goodbyes and began to make her rounds. After all, it would be impolite to just bounce, but right when she was about to finish, a gentle hand brushed against her arm.

"Yes?" she asked, expecting to turn and see a PA telling her she forgot something, or perhaps someone asking for a selfie. Except it wasn't anything like that at all.

"Ben!" she cried, a smile breaking out across her features. "What are you doing in LA? Where are the kids!?"

"Missy and Dani are watching them, don't worry. They're all very excited to have a sleepover party in the main house with their cousins and Aunties."

"I can't believe it. You flew all the way out here for me?"

"I did. I figure we can have a lovely dinner together tonight, maybe see some sights tomorrow, then take an overnight flight back home."

Chastity couldn't believe it. Throwing her arms around his neck, she peppered his face with kisses. "You're incredible, you know that?"

"Aw, y'all better stop being so adorable or I'm going to have to ask you to leave."

Chastity looked to one of the two main hosts, who was standing a bit away and looking entirely amused. Chastity wasn't embarrassed though. She'd spent far too much of her life running away from the love of her life to waste even a moment being bashful about it.

"Sorry, an unfortunate side effect of being in love means we're adorable all the time."

"Hah! I need to go home and tell my wife that." He laughed good-naturedly, as did his co-host who was approaching. The two were funny like that. The latter, a tall man with a reddish beard, didn't even know what was going on, but if his friend was laughing, he was too.

Either that or he had exceptional hearing. It was a coin toss, basically.

"Thank you again for filming with us, Chastity. We really appreciate you taking the time, especially since it involves being away from your family."

"Oh, don't worry about that," she answered with a sappy grin. "Turns out my family came to me."

CHASTITY HELD Ben's hand from across the table as they lovingly stared at it other. It was sappy. It was cheesy. And it was oh so perfect.

Sometimes she bemoaned the decade that they'd spent apart, but she'd always remind herself that it was that time that allowed them to develop their personalities and become the people they needed to be to come together in the end.

But still, it would have been nice not to have been so alone that whole time.

"When was the last time we had a romantic dinner with just the two of us?" she mused, squeezing his hand. It was an old habit, the sort of fakey Morse code that they would squeeze into each other's palm, but Chastity loved it. A percussive sort of reminder of just how much they meant to each other.

"It's certainly been a while. Maybe before Danny's last birthday?"

"Sounds about right."

"We should try to make a better habit of that."

"We absolutely should."

Strange, how easy it was for time to get away from them. Marrying into the Millers had certainly changed Chastity's life. Suddenly money was never an issue, and she was free to pursue the career she'd dreamed of. But even with pretty much everything she'd ever wanted, too often she found herself falling into the rhythm of work, sleep, manage the kids, manage the next social event, cook food and eat. And that was with Ma Miller insisting that she continue to make dinner at her house for anyone who wanted to drop in. Somehow, there was always enough, which seemed particularly impossible, but was true nonetheless.

But she had Ben in front of her for the moment, and she wasn't going to take it for granted.

"I love you," she murmured, beaming dopily at him.

"I love you too, sweetheart."

Chastity didn't care that they were in a restaurant. She leaned forward and captured his lips with hers, hoping he could feel just how much he made her heart swell. She had no doubt that she and Ben had been meant for each other. She'd found the love of her life and couldn't be more grateful.

When they parted, Ben had that dazed look on his face he had whenever she kissed him especially well, and Chastity sat back in satisfaction.

Their server came soon after that, and they ordered their drink and an appetizer before returning their attention to each other. But before they could start up a conversation, Ben's phone rang.

"Oh, it's one of my cousins from New Mexico," he said, eyebrows shooting up. "They never call. Do you mind if I take this?"

"Is it the cousin with the name that sounds like mine?"

"Charity? No, it's Cassidy, the second eldest."

"Of course, you can answer, dear. I was just being a bit cheeky."

"Right, sorry. Little bit of jet lag still."

"It's alright; you don't have to deny that my kiss left you off-kilter. It's not the first time."

He huffed a laugh then answered, asking if it was important and explaining he was on a date. Even though the timing wasn't convenient, Chastity couldn't help but rest her chin in her hand and just *look* at her husband.

He was ruggedly handsome, but at the same time, boyishly cute. From the earnest smile he had from talking to a family member, to the hearty laugh he let out—no doubt Cassidy said something particularly snarky. Chastity couldn't help but think about how her son Danny had his father's chin through and through. She wondered; would little Dakota have his brows? Daniella his laugh? To her, they all looked so much like him, but that didn't bother her. She loved seeing his reflection in them just as much as she loved that they were individual beings with their own lives and wants. And she loved that she was getting to watch them grow up with him.

She was so caught up in emotions; it was like being in her twenties again. Her heart picked up and the blood rushed to her cheeks. When Ben finally hung up the phone, there was no stopping her mouth as it moved of its own accord.

"Sorry about that. Apparently, there's—"

"I want another baby."

That froze him still and he looked at her, eyes wide. "Pardon?"

"Uh, I mean, if that's alright with you. No, I mean…" She took a deep breath, trying to gather herself. "Ben, would you like to have another baby with me?"

She wasn't 100% sure how he would react. After all, she had to admit that it was pretty out of the blue. But then Ben's expression grew soft and his other hand reached out to stroke her cheek.

"I would love that."

Oh. Even after so many years together, he still knew exactly what to say to make her swoon.

"It's a plan then."

"It most certainly is."

3

Bart

"And that's when I knew I needed to get my life together. It wasn't going to be overnight, and I was aware that there were going to be pitfalls and setbacks. But if I wanted to be with the woman I was madly in love with, I had to make sure I was at least trying to be worthy of her."

There was a chorus of affirmative sounds around them and Bart finished up with his speech. He still wasn't much of a guy for public speaking, but as he'd continued to develop his role with the VA support group, he'd learned it was a part of the position.

"So that's when I made a promise. To be the best me I could possibly be. It means a lot of different things, but for us, it's being mindful of my mood and mental health. It's getting to my appointments on time. And it's making sure I always communicate with her. If I need my space, I have to tell her. If I need extra support, I tell her that too.

"I'm the luckiest man on earth, or at least that's how it feels. And it's thanks to a lot of the help here at the VA that I'm standing here before you."

He swallowed, nearing the end of his speech. He could feel apprehension rising along his spine, which meant he needed to hurry it along.

He'd come a long way since that first time Missy had found him alone in the middle of the night. But he still had his pitfalls. Anxiety was his biggest one, as it was the most likely to trigger a sleepwalking episode or panic attack.

"So remember that you're not alone here. Talk to your sponsor, make friends. We have plenty of resources to make sure that no man is ever left behind. I won't pretend that I know all of your troubles, but I do know that we can all conquer them together."

With one last nod, Bart returned to his seat. There was a smattering of applause, but it was quiet. The meeting wasn't exactly the place for loud noises or cheer. And Bart preferred it that way. He didn't see himself as a hero. He was just a guy trying to do his best in the world.

The next speaker went up and Bart allowed himself to zone out a little, recovering from what had been a very long week. But still, he was happy that they were able to expand their support group even further.

It was a tenuous balance, trying to make sure everyone who needed help got it, but also that they didn't get so big that people slipped through the cracks. Because that was one of the biggest threats to vets everywhere. It was so easy for them to be ignored. Forgotten. Lost in paperwork and bureaucracy.

Bart was just trying to do his best to make sure that stopped happening. At least in his little corner of the world.

Eventually, the meeting wrapped up, and then came most people's favorite part: the social hour. It wasn't really an hour, and Bart still wasn't very social, but it was a thirty-to-forty-minute chance for people to snack on food, drink coffee, and make connections that might be important to them later.

Bart did his best to look approachable. Missy had been working with him on that for quite a while, but his default expression did tend to lean more towards cloudy than welcoming. But he wanted to be there in case anybody in need wanted to talk to him.

Despite being a bit of a hermit, he was well aware that his story had spread to a lot of the town. And they certainly had added plenty of myth to it. While he wasn't thrilled with their additions, he didn't mind that his reputation helped draw other wounded people to him for help.

So, when a young man in a wheelchair rolled over to talk to Bart about dealing with wait times and medical red tape, he didn't mind coaching the soldier and giving him some references for people who could advocate for his medical needs. And he didn't mind helping the woman after that.

But after this third or so conversation, he realized that more time had passed than he thought, and Missy was supposed to be picking him up.

Bart could drive fine all by himself, but over the years he'd found that he preferred not to drive at night if he could arrange not to. It was too easy to get lost in the highway hypnosis and end up back in Afghanistan, lost in the sands. It didn't happen every time, but Missy—saint that she was—said she didn't mind being his chauffeur for support meetings that ran later in the evening.

Sure, maybe some of the soldiers around him would find it strange that he was more comfortable riding passenger side in their mommy mobile, aka the cobalt blue minivan they'd purchased after the birth of their second child, but Bart couldn't care less.

What he did care about, however, was keeping her waiting outside for *forty-five minutes.*

Bart was a timely person, or at least he liked to think so. Which made him wonder why Missy hadn't called him. If he just didn't appear outside the building, he couldn't help but think that she'd know something was wrong.

"You're kidding, a whole horse?"

"I would never kid about horses, actually."

Bart's head went from his phone towards the all too familiar voice. Sure enough, there she was, standing with two female veterans that Bart loosely knew.

"That's amazing. Say, you need hands with that operation? Sounds pretty intense."

"We can always use volunteers!" Missy said happily, pulling out her wallet and handing the woman a card. "Soldiers from Bart's support groups get preference, actually. And we do have career opportunities, if you end up loving the work."

"Wow, well that's good to hear. I've always loved animals."

"And our animals need all the love they can get. I've actually been building a network of a dozen or so different rescues and conservatories, so we've got a lot of rehabilitation, clean up, and pretty much everything else you can imagine to do."

Bart had to look at Missy as she grinned, making friends much easier than he ever could. Even after all their years together, she still shined in his eyes. Sure, there were some stress lines on her face. But she was still gorgeous, full of life and passion that encouraged him to be better. To always improve himself.

There were bad days, sure, but that didn't matter. What mattered was constantly moving forward. Improving, learning, growing, healing. And Missy helped him do exactly that.

Finally, her eyes drifted from the two she was talking to and connected with his. Electricity jolted through him, and he was just as helplessly enraptured by her as he had been when she'd been a floating light in his dreams.

She grinned, and it was like the whole room illuminated. And she continued to glow as she approached him, gripping his hand.

"Hey there, handsome. Good to see you."

"Sorry for running behind. I didn't realize the time."

"That's alright. I figured you were doing important work."

"Thank you for understanding."

She leaned in and kissed his cheek. "I'm so proud of you, babe. Now, shall we go home?"

"Yeah, I'm definitely ready."

With a few last goodbyes, they headed out to where Missy had parked. Getting in, Bart couldn't help but watch his wife as she got into the driver's seat.

"What?" she murmured, catching his stare. "Is there something on my face?"

"Nah. Just thinking that I'm the luckiest man in the world."

"Awww," she said, expression going syrupy. "Aren't you sweet."

"Just saying the truth."

She leaned over a moment, pressing another kiss to his other cheek, before buckling herself in.

"Ready?"

"Ready," he replied, feeling warm and safe. As he always did around Missy.

He was going home, and that was the only place he wanted to be.

4

Missy

Missy grunted as she picked up one of the rocks she was hauling and set it down into the bottom of the watering hole she was constructing. The conservation park she was helping at in Florida really needed this set up for their animals.

"Hey, have you had water yet?"

Blinking the sweat out of her eyes, Missy looked up to see Annabelle, one of the workers she'd gotten to know while visiting the conservatory down in Florida. She was a nice girl, and a great helper even though she was so tiny. When Missy had first met her, she'd been surprised to find out that the petite woman was twenty-five. She wasn't quite five foot and had to barely weigh a hundred pounds.

"Yeah, I've been hydrating. Had a sports drink too to replace my electrolytes."

"Oh, awesome! Are you gonna be here when I get back from my break?"

"Yeah. And then if you'll help me pack up, I'll head home."

"Sounds good to me!"

Well, it wasn't really home. Not at all. It was a small hotel that was only a twenty-minute drive from the conservatory and where she was staying for her month-long visit.

Missy had never expected to end up so hands-on at the Everglades Conservation Park, but that was often how her life went. She'd first contacted them after seeing an emergency post they'd put on social media after a hurricane had severely damaged several parts of their small operation. She'd helped them through that, then kept in contact.

Somehow, that had turned into her coming down and helping a couple years later when they messaged her about advice on their expansion. And when Missy offered to help, she really meant it. Sure, she probably could have stayed in their office and done all the desk duty that could really bog down rescues and the like, but the park desperately needed manpower.

Besides, she could use the workout. Her friend Ginny had started MMA lessons in the city and had been beating Missy way more than vise versa lately, and that just wouldn't do. Missy had a reputation to maintain, after all. As well as impressive biceps.

She missed her family though. She went on trips often, a necessity given her involvement with so many different charities, but never one so long. She'd wanted to have it only be two weeks, but on her first day of visiting Florida, she'd realized that they needed way more help than fourteen days would allow.

"Come on, rock, work with me," Missy grumbled, trying to

force the thing into place. She'd sealed the bottom of the water pit, but she'd found that leaving it that way left it looking far too artificial. Some animals were fine with that, but too many found it alien, uncomfortable, and that lowered their happiness or willingness to engage.

Eventually, the rock slid into place, and she was able to move on to the next one. And the next one. In one of life's perfect timings, Annabelle arrived just as she was finishing up, helping her with the last couple of stones. After that, they took all of the supplies and hauled them to the shed.

"You know, I really appreciate you getting so down and dirty here," the small woman said as they closed up the northern supply shed. "When I heard that some head honcho from out west was coming, I thought you'd be a real desk jockey. Or maybe even look down on us."

"Why would I do that?"

"Aw, you know. We don't have the most money. We're not like some of those famous conservation parks that have everything you could want and then some."

"Nah, everyone's gotta start somewhere, and I'm just glad that you're all here. Teaching Esmerelda and Jennifer how to apply for more grants should also help."

"I can't believe how many you knew about!"

"Well, when you've been at it as long as I have."

"And how long *is* that?"

Missy paused, thinking for a moment. It seemed like a lifetime ago when Bart introduced her to her first rescue as one of the most thoughtful gifts she'd ever received. She'd kept it small for a long while—a little over a year—before she started her fundraiser to save wild horses. That had been a joint effort with Chastity's tribe on the reservation and really was what kicked off her contact with other projects for joint ventures.

"Geez, almost six years now."

When did she get so old? For more than half a decade passing and having two kids, she still felt pretty spry. Granted, that could have been from her mostly trying to keep up with Ginny. Her fighting counterpart hadn't had any children yet, so she had far more time than Missy.

"Wow, six years. I'll be twenty-eight then. It's hard to imagine myself in the future."

"Your twenties go fast, trust me."

"Wait, you're *not* in your twenties?"

"Huh? No, I'm in my thirties. I did just mention that I've been at this for six years."

"Yeah, I thought you were some sort of teenage or fresh-out-of-college prodigy."

"Oh no, hardly. I didn't really get started till around my mid-twenties. I've just learned a whole lot real fast. Plus I worked as a vet tech assistant for a good long while before that."

"Wow, well I think that's so cool," Annabelle said.

They finished the last of their work and Annabelle untied her bandana from her neck to wipe the sweat from her face. Missy made a note that she could use something like that. Sure, it got hot during the summers back home plenty, but the humidity of Florida was killing her.

"I'm gonna head off now. You gon' be alright?" Missy asked.

"Oh yeah, I'm gonna finish up with some of the pathing on the south side, check in with Esmerelda and then go home."

"Sounds like a plan. I'll see you tomorrow."

"See ya tomorrow, Mrs. Miller."

"Please, call me Missy."

The younger woman narrowed her eyes. "That feels wrong."

"You'll get used to it, trust me. A lot faster than I'll ever get used to being called Mrs. Miller." In Missy's head, that would always belong to her mother-in-law.

"Alright then, Miss Missy..." Annabelle squinted further. "I'll work on it."

"You do you," Missy said with a half-salute before heading off. It wasn't the longest walk back to her Jeep, but she was still exhausted when she slid in. She needed a good shower and a long sleep. If she had any luck, maybe she would be able to get a video call in with Bart.

They did their best to contact each other every day, but considering it was summer and he had both of the kids, that contact was usually condensed down to "I love you" texts. She only had a week and a half left before she would be heading back home and able to see him again, but those ten days seemed like an awful long time.

An impossibly long time.

She'd never been away from home for so long. Her rule was two weeks max, and any projects that needed longer than that would have to be broken up into chunks. She wasn't upset that she'd made an exception for Everglades Conservation Park, but it was definitely testing her limits.

Back aching, skin stinging from sweat, and hands throbbing, she pulled into the small hotel she'd chosen. It wasn't a run-down place by any means, but it was a Mom n' Pop. And that did Missy just fine.

Exhaustion weighing down her frame, Missy slid her card and entered. With her mind far away, she didn't even realize the lights were on until three people were yelling at her.

"*Surprise!!!*"

Missy yelped, jumping back with her fists raised, before she recognized the familiar faces.

"Bart?" she said, eyes wide. "What are you doing here?"

"We missed you so badly that we figured we'd swing by."

Swing by to Florida. Which was states away. How quintessentially Miller of him.

"Mommy!"

Gabriel and Ginger both ran up to her, tackling her into a hug. It amazed her how much they'd grown. It felt like just last month that she'd held them in her arms, all swaddled up like a precious little bundle. They were only a year and a half apart, and they just kept growing. She hadn't planned on stopping at two kids, but she hadn't really planned them either. Bart and her had decided to just let their bodies do what their bodies wanted to do, and apparently that was a pair of little ones.

Still... Missy wouldn't mind another. Maybe if she slowed down a little, her body would catch on.

"Hey, my babies. I missed you."

"We missed you too!"

Bart, the patient saint that he was, let her kids hug her for a good long while before clearing his throat. Missy extricated herself from her kids and went right to his open arms.

Instantly, she could feel her entire body relax at the contact. His scent filled her nose, and he was so strong and sure against her. Even after so many years together, she still felt safest in his arms. The whole world could be against them, but she would be alright as long as they had their little family.

"I love you," he murmured against the top of her head. Heart thrumming, Missy tilted her head up. He got the message instantly and dipped his head down to kiss her.

"Ewwww! Gross!" That was Gabriel, of course. Her son was just old enough to have gotten to the girls-are-icky stage.

"Shhh, be nice!" And that was his sister, the older one who was more aware of what it meant to be polite.

But Missy loved them both fiercely for it, even though Bart and her had to break apart to chuckle at their kids.

"I love you too," she murmured back, grinning like a madwoman at her love. And in that small hotel room, covered in the sweat of the day and surrounded by the beautiful family that they'd built together, she couldn't help but feel like the luckiest woman in the world.

5

Benji

*B*enji secured the last shingle on the edge of the roof, feeling satisfaction run through him at a job well done.

"Not bad, if I do say so myself."

There was still plenty of work to be done on the expansion to his and Dani's house, but the framework and exterior was finally done. Thank goodness. Not that Benji didn't enjoy the process, but he was ready to move forward with their life together and keep growing their family.

When he'd first built their little home away from the manor on the edge of the property, he'd thought he'd made enough room for them to be set a good long while. But after they'd had their first little one, they'd quickly realized that if they wanted to keep growing their family, they needed way more room.

Climbing down the ladder he'd set up earlier, he went around to the front of the house. With all the construction muck and grit on his boots, he made sure to sit down outside the door and take his boots off before stepping in. But as he sat, he could hear a low voice slowly rumbling at a relaxing beat.

Ah, his brother Ben must have been reading to little Charlie. That made sense; it was almost nap time. Normally it would be Dani taking care of him while Benji was working on the house. But there was a lot going on with her family and she'd been doing more things on their home ranch lately.

That was the wonderful thing about having such a close-knit family, in Benji's opinion. They were always there for each other, no matter what happened.

"And when the hare asked the tortoise how he could have possibly won, the tortoise told him that 'slow and steady wins the race.'"

"Turty!"

"Yup, that's the tortoise there, talking to the bunbun."

Perhaps other people would find it odd to hear Ben using such a sweet, soft tone, but Benji was more than used to it. The truth was, Benedict Miller was a complete and total softy when it came to kids. He was always the first to offer to babysit and also the first to crumble under good puppy dog eyes. He knew to put his foot down when it came to spoiling any of them, but he also was the most likely to indulge them.

"Perfect timing," Benji said, finally stepping in and putting on his house slippers. "You ready for nap time now, Charlie boy?"

Charlie didn't say anything, instead just nodding and lifting his hands for Benji to pick him up. He wasn't the most verbal, but that was alright. Benji always understood what he meant, even without a word between them.

"You want a drink before you tuck in?" Benji asked, taking his son into his arms. Charlie nodded, holding three fingers up to his mouth like the letter W. It was one of the several ASL signs he knew. "Some water? Okay, I can do that, but you have to make sure that you go potty before you go to nap, okay?"

Another nod.

"Alright, let's just say goodbye to Uncle Benny, okay?" Benji looked to his brother, who was already standing up. "You okay swinging by tomorrow too?"

"Yeah, how's Dani holding up?"

"She's doing alright. Things are just hectic back at her home. Apparently, her brother's having some trouble."

"That's rough. That fire happened so long ago. It's strange to think that it's still affecting them."

"Yeah, it was pretty bad. They were in a coma for a while, and then there was a lot of rehabilitation, and some infections set them back. I think that's what's going on now."

"Ugh, well, whenever you need babysitting, I'm your guy."

"Gotcha. Thanks again, for everything."

"Of course, what else is family for?"

"Bye-bye, Unka!"

"See ya later, Charlie!"

Ben headed out, and Benji went through the normal naptime routine of getting Charlie water and making sure he went to the bathroom. Thankfully, their little boy was always a great sleeper. He'd probably be out for two hours and still able to go to sleep at night.

Once he was tucked in, Benji went back downstairs and looked around. The house seemed strangely empty without Dani. She brought so much life to their home, filling it with beautiful songs or silly little ditties while she went about her day.

Goodness, he loved her. He loved her so much that it hurt sometimes, but in the best way possible. In the years they'd been together, he felt like they'd grown closer than ever, becoming the best versions of themselves.

...he wished that Dani was home.

Well, he could at least occupy himself with loading the dishwasher. He wasn't the biggest fan of the chore, but his policy was that if Dani cooked for him, it was his job to clean up after her. He was all about even distribution of effort. He wasn't exactly the most researched when it came to psychology or all that, but he remembered reading an article while in the OBGYN's waiting room with Dani about how women often had to spend 54% more time doing chores than their partners even while working outside of the home, and that had always stuck with him. So, he did his best to make sure he helped wherever he could, whether it was with their son, the house, or her family.

He was just finishing up with his task when he heard wheels crunching up their small drive. Chore instantly forgotten, he practically ran to the front door and threw it open.

"Well, aren't you a sight for sore eyes," Dani said, wearily striding towards him.

Did he mention that he loved her? Because he did. It swelled up in his chest and made him want to reach for her.

So he did just that. He grabbed her the moment she was in the door, wrapping his arms around her and crashing his lips to hers. His body rushed with the feel of her, joy, attraction, relief all flooding his system. After so many years together, one would think that kissing wouldn't affect him so, but it still did.

When they parted, they were both breathing a bit raggedly, and Dani was giving him that hazy look that made his blood light up.

"Whoa, what was that for?" she asked, her tone dreamy.

"I missed you."

"I was only gone for the weekend."

"And that was a weekend too long," he replied before capturing her lips again. His hands roved over her until they settled at her waist and hauled her up.

She'd told him plenty of times it baffled her why he liked to set her on different surfaces. The kitchen counter, the dining room table, his workbench. Benji couldn't quite put a finger on it, but he suspected it was a cross section of feeling strong and masculine, along with the way her cheeks would always flush so prettily.

And as he carried her over to the closest counter, setting her on it, she flushed just like he hoped. Pretty, pretty pink rose from her neck all the way up to her forehead, and he wondered if it was scientifically possible for the vibrant color to seep into her hair.

He kissed her ragged, hoping she could feel how much he missed her and how much she mattered to him. He still wasn't the best at words, but he liked to think that he was pretty good at loving his soulmate.

He did have to come back for air eventually, and when he did, he rested his forehead against hers. Their breathing mingled, and he felt so connected with her.

"Did something happen?" Dani asked, caressing his face.

"I finished the roof."

Her eyes went wide. "What? Really? That's amazing!" She gave each of his cheeks a peck before her brow furrowed. "And that made you want to kiss me senseless? Don't get me wrong, I'm not complaining, but I don't exactly see the correlation."

"Well, I guess you could say that it got me thinking about exactly what we're building the expansion for."

Dani's eyes flashed at that, and she looked at him with that same hunger that always made him feel like he was the center of the world. "Oh, is *that* what's going on?"

He nodded, feeling himself blush. They were just a couple of tomato-heads, the both of them, but he loved it. "Yeah, that might be what's going on."

"Where's Charlie? Is he down for a nap?"

"Yup, sleeping soundly."

A slow, saucy smile spread across Dani's features. "Hey, wanna go upstairs with me?"

Benji couldn't help but mirror her grin. Goodness, he loved his wife. "I'd like that a lot."

Hand in hand, they ran up the stairs like newlyweds, giggling softly and drunk on each other. And Benji wouldn't have it any other way.

6

Dani

*D*ani held her breath as the doctor finished securing the last of the straps of her brother's prosthetic. While her elder brother had been able to keep all of his limbs but a single finger, the middle Touhey child hadn't been so lucky. A bad infection during the second year of recovery had caused an emergency amputation of his leg, and the path to healing from that had been a long one.

But finally, after waiting seemingly forever, he had the approval of his physical therapist and his doctors to get his prosthetic. That hadn't exactly been a short process either, between fittings, casings, and everything else.

"Are you ready?" his physical therapist said, holding out both of her arms for the man to grasp.

"As ready as I'll ever be."

"Alright, here we go."

There was a tense moment as he slowly rose from his chair, gripping his physical therapist like his life depended on it. And then, for the first time in over a year, Dani's brother stood on his own two feet.

"You did it!" Dani cried, unable to help it when her voice went shrill. What could she say? She was so happy that it could practically burst out of her skin.

"That's my boy!"

"Oh, look at you! Just look at you!"

"Yeah, look at you go!"

It was probably pretty overwhelming for the whole family to exclaim something at once, but they all had been waiting so long for James to have his leg that it felt like Christmas, a birthday, and an anniversary all wrapped into one.

"You're amazing," Chester said, striding forward. But the physical therapist held out a hand to stop him.

"Let him finish his walk first, and then we can get on with the congratulations."

"Right, sorry."

"Don't worry about it," James said, although his voice was strained.

Dani was breathless as she watched her older brother take one tiny step. Then another. She was elated, yes, but worry also lanced through her. What if he fell? What if the leg collapsed? What if, what if, what if?

As if he could sense her mounting concern, Benji slid his hand into hers, silently squeezing. It helped calm her, and Dani couldn't be more grateful that he was there. As an honorary Touhey, he certainly helped her feel more tethered and less likely to get swept away in the torrent of panic.

"It's gonna be okay," he whispered, pressing a kiss to the top of her head.

Dani leaned into his side, watching as James took yet another step. Then one more before he gasped.

"Yeah, I think that's good for the day," he wheezed, face flushed and sweat already dribbling down his brow. The nurse that was present quickly scooted his chair back under him, and he sat with a thud. "Whew! That was... that was really something."

"You're incredible," Dani said, rushing forward with Chester to hug him. He tolerated their affection a few beats before shrugging them both off.

"Alright, alright, that's enough for now. I'm pretty jazzed too. Now my budding career of doing the two-step can finally come to fruition."

"Yeah, because this is what was holding you back," Benji said, coming forward to put a supportive hand on James' shoulder.

"Exactly, it's just straight shootin' now."

There was a bit of laughter between them, but then they all parted for their parents to come through and give their own little bits of affection. James handled it very well, for what it was worth. Dani knew he didn't really like being the center of attention, so she appreciated that he was indulging all of them.

"Now, there's still a long way to go before you're back to full mobility," the doctor said. "But this is an excellent start. We'll need to start scheduling more physical therapy appointments, and I want to go over properly taking care of your skin. There can be some issues with contact dermatitis or abrasion."

"Yeah, I gotcha," James said, cracking a weary grin. "Whatever we need to get me back on my feet again. Hah! *Feet.* I never thought that would be an exciting plural for me."

Dani could feel herself tearing up, and in the back of her mind, she knew that one of the reasons he had such great medical care along with a state-of-the-art prosthetic was because of Benji's money. His family really had done a lot for them since the fire, and being married to a multi-millionaire-slash-kinda-billionaire had really eliminated a lot of her stresses in life. Not all of them, but a whole lot.

Dani shuddered to think what position they'd be in with their old insurance and budget, but that just led her to wonder what other people did. Was there something that could be done about that? Giving resources to those who needed them and didn't have the right access?

She didn't know, but it certainly was something to think about.

"What'cha got on your mind?" Benji asked, hooking his arm through hers.

"Just the future," Dani said, giving him a teary smile. "Always the future."

"Sounds grand," he replied, grinning at her brightly. "As long as we're together."

7

Bradley

*B*radley twirled Sophia under his arm, kicking out his leg, then twirling her right back. The end of the song was a wild crescendo, and he could feel his heart in his chest as they finished it out.

"Whew!" Sophia said once it was done, brushing her bangs out of her face. She'd started growing her hair out after their wedding, and he had to admit it looked good on her. "Wanna go sit a spell?"

"Yep," Bradley answered, just as breathless. "Probably should have quit on the last round, but I couldn't pass up on that song."

"It was a good one," Sophia agreed, taking his hand in hers as they walked back to their table. "But not bad for a couple of newcomers."

"We've been doing this for five months. I think we might not be newcomers anymore."

"Eh, I still feel like it. But maybe it's just because this is the latest hobby on my list."

"How are you doing on that, by the way?"

"About halfway through it, actually, can you believe it?"

"With your determination? Yes, I can."

Sophia's cheeks colored slightly, but Bradley couldn't help but smile. Ever since her ex had been completely removed from her life, Sophia had put together a list of all the things that she wanted to try but he had always told her she couldn't. It was an impressive collection of things, from wearing a two-piece bathing suit to rock climbing, to ordering something above thirteen dollars at a nice restaurant that she paid for herself.

Sometimes it made Bradley's fist still curl when he thought of all the awful things Sophia had had to endure, how much she was mistreated, and all the good things that had been stolen from her. But watching her blossom into someone unaffected by the specter of her ex was a wonderful thing indeed.

"Ho boy, that was certainly a whirlwind, wasn't it?"

Bradley ripped his eyes away from his love to see another couple had joined them at their table, equally breathless and red-cheeked.

"Yeah, it's one of their wilder songs," he agreed.

"Have y'all been doing this long? This is only our second dance get-together."

"About half a year," Bradley answered. "It's been a lot of fun!"

"Oh, I bet! And what a good workout!" The woman paused to pour herself a glass of water from the pitcher on the table.

"It's great cardio," Sophia said with a nod. It was a small thing, but Bradley couldn't help but be proud of her yet again. It hadn't been all that long ago that she wouldn't be able to talk to strangers without a lot of time beforehand to prep. It really was amazing how far she'd come.

"By the way, I'm Cleetus and this is my wife, Maribelle," the husband said, grinning broadly. Those were certainly some old-fashioned names. Bradley added them to his mental list of baby possibilities for the future. He didn't know how far in the future, but he had hope.

Considering everything that Sophia had gone through, and the stranglehold her ex had had over her, Bradley understood that she wasn't ready for children. He didn't think he was either. Not yet. Not when he was still enjoying getting to know who his wife was without a shadow of terror over her.

But that didn't mean he *never* wanted kids. In fact, the more time that passed, the more it seemed like a possible reality rather than a far-off dream. They'd been married a little over a year, after all, and he could envision them starting their family somewhere around the third or so.

"I'm Bradley, and this is Sophia."

"Nice to meet ya! Y'all a couple of married fogies too?"

"Yup, we are," Sophia said, grinning brightly. Bradley would be lying if he said he wasn't affected by how happy she looked at the statement. As much as he felt like an exceedingly lucky man for being able to capture the heart of such an amazing woman, it actually made him feel pretty complimented that she was so pleased to be married to *him*. "A little over a year."

"Ooooh, so still in the honeymoon phase!"

Bradley grinned wanly at that. If they knew he and Sophia had been engaged for over two years while she lived with his family, maybe they wouldn't think that. But he didn't feel the need to go into detail about Sophia's past with strangers, even if they were plenty polite.

"Yeah, hah, still on our honeymoon."

"How'd y'all meet?"

Ah, there it was, the question he didn't really want to answer. But he supposed it would be rude to shut down right then and there.

"Ah, it's a long story," he answered with a shrug.

But to his great surprise, it was Sophia who answered.

"Basically, Bradley here showed up like a knight in shining armor and whisked me right off my feet."

"Oh really now?" Maribelle said, resting her chin in her hand. "Sounds romantic."

"It was and is. I wasn't in the greatest spot, and he just swooped in like it was the easiest thing. Even chased off a bad ex of mine that wouldn't give me up.

"I wouldn't be here right now if it weren't for him. So yeah, I don't know if we'll ever get out of the honeymoon phase, and I'm just fine with that."

"Wow," Cleetus remarked, letting out a chuckle. "That's certainly a story."

Bradley, however, could only stare at her. She made it sound like he'd ridden in on a horse and was completely in control of the situation instead of accidentally stumbling on her ex-fiancé trying to force her back home with him. Or that he hadn't bumbled through a fake engagement to her as he tried to buy her time.

As he sat there, more than a little dumbfounded, another lively song started up. Bradley hadn't even known he liked swing music before they'd started attending the dancing get-togethers, and if he weren't so gobsmacked by her, he might have even been able to recognize the song.

"Well, that's our cue to get back on the floor," Maribelle said, grabbing her husband's hand and pulling him up from the table. The two hurried off, leaving Bradley and Sophia all alone.

"What?" she asked, noticing his stare.

"Do you really see me that way?" he asked, unable to hide his wide eyes and shocked expression.

"Like what?"

"Like some hero that came in and saved the day."

Now it was her turn to give him a quizzical look. "Isn't that what happened?"

"I, uh, I what now?"

She reached across the table and gently took his hand in hers, the expression in her dark eyes earnest. "Bradley, I was trapped in my situation. I tried as hard as I could to get out of it on my own, but he had the resources and support that I didn't. Without you and your family, he would have collected me that night and taken me back. I honestly don't even know if I would be alive."

Bradley's mouth fell open ever so slightly. He'd known that Sophia had been in danger with her ex. He'd been by her side as she went through the entire legal process, listening to testimony from her and several other young women who he'd targeted. But Bradley had never stopped to think that she'd actually been in mortal danger.

But that was the case, wasn't it?

He could have lost her before their story ever started. And that would be a real shame, because Sophia was one of the most amazing additions to the world. She was creative, kind, hilarious, and had a fiery sort of determination that always inspired Bradley to be better. To do better.

"I guess I don't say it enough, Bradley, but I owe you my life. And I intend to spend the rest of it showing you how grateful I am and how much I love you."

Bradley didn't expect to get choked up in the middle of a swing dance get-together, but his life was pretty good at taking unpredictable paths. Swallowing hard, he leaned in and captured Sophia's lips in his.

It was a gentle kiss, as most of theirs were. Soft, sweet, and lingering. When they parted, Sophia beamed at him again, her smile dazzling.

"Ya wanna go dance, husband?" she murmured, offering her small hand.

"I would," he answered, taking hers and mirroring her happy expression. Together they flitted over to the dance floor, and Bradley picked her up, swinging her around as they got into the music. And while she twirled, he couldn't help but be excited for whatever adventure they went on next.

8

Sophia

"Hyah!"

Sophia brought her arm up to block her opponent's punch, then swept her leg forward in a half-circle in an attempt to catch their calf. They managed to evade her, however, and reset their positions.

Concentrate, Sophia. Keep your mind clear.

Easier thought than done, but Sophia had been training for months to be ready for her dojo's Martial Arts tournament. She wanted to do her *sensei* proud.

When she was younger, she had been far too poor to ever afford something like that. And then, when she'd been with her ex, he would never allow such a thing. But Bradley, her wonderful husband, encouraged all of her strange ventures, from baking classes to swing dancing to MMA and some jujitsu on the side.

He was wonderful, a dream come true. And although it had taken her quite a while to fully trust him, she couldn't be happier that she did.

She knew he was in the audience, and she wanted to do him proud. Granted, he would be proud of her no matter what, but still, it was the principle of it all.

Her opponent went in for a kick, which Sophia caught. Tucking it under her arm, she rolled into a takedown, pinning her opponent as they landed. They fought her hold, they fought *hard,* but Sophia held on until finally, they tapped out of her lock.

And just like that, she won.

It didn't hit her right away. She scrambled to her feet and offered a hand to her defeated opponent, and the woman took it.

"Good match. You did really well."

"Thank you," Sofia answered, catching her breath. "You weren't half bad yourself."

Their conversation was cut short as the ref came over and lifted Sophia's hand, declaring her the winner. There was mild cheering from the crowd; she wasn't the main event after all. Most of the people were there to see the male welter and heavy weights.

But there was one particular section of the crowd that went absolutely wild, cheering and hollering like they'd just won the lottery. Sophia didn't have to look in their direction to know that it was a good number of the Millers who'd come out to see her do her best.

And apparently the best was winning her weight division in the novice female category. Not bad for only being at it a little over a year.

Everything kind of became a blur as she made her way off the mat and towards the locker rooms. She made it about halfway there before strong arms enveloped her, picking her up and swinging her around.

"You did it!"

If it were anybody else, she might have struck them or flipped them over her shoulder. But she recognized her husband's cologne, and she instantly relaxed in his arms.

"I can't believe that happened," she said as he set her down.

"I sure can," Bradley said, turning her so he could pepper her face with kisses. Sophia giggled at how much it tickled her, and she was more than amused by the juxtaposition of her going from fighting tooth and nail with an opponent in the ring to laughing giddily with her husband. "You've been working so hard."

"Hey, at least all those lessons are paying off," she said, letting him pull her close to his chest in a fierce hug.

There had been a time, not too long ago, when she thought she would be alone forever. That no one would ever be able to help her, and she'd live constantly in the shadow of the man she feared most. But Bradley had brought out the sun. Their coming together hadn't been flawless, and they'd both fumbled, but she knew without a doubt that he was her soulmate.

And maybe he'd be the father of her children?

It was a heady thought, and it made her heart thunder in her chest. For a long time, she hadn't wanted anything to do with pregnancy. Not since her ex-fiancé had been trying to trap her by getting her pregnant, locking her to his side forever, and she couldn't let that happen.

So naturally, she'd been pretty uncomfortable with the idea. But time had passed, and she felt more secure than she ever had in her entire life. Plus, she knew that she was completely in love with Bradley and he with her. A real love, not the controlling, awful thing she'd experienced before.

Then again, she'd have to stop with all of her hobbies, so maybe not quite yet. She had several more to check off her list.

"They're paying off as long as you enjoy them," he replied, kissing her cheek as the rest of his clan caught up with them. Except they weren't just his clan, they were hers too. She'd lived with them throughout the years that it took for her to get through the trial and put her past behind her, becoming pretty much as family as one could get. It was nice, and that security had allowed her to reconnect with the biological one that she'd been isolated from.

"Sweetie, you did so good!" That was Mama Miller, who joined in on the hug.

"That was pretty impressive, shortstop." That was Benji, of course, who gave her a wink. They hadn't interacted that much when she'd first joined the ranch, but since then, they'd definitely developed a big brother, little sister sort of dynamic. "Remind me not to ever make you angry."

"That's right," she answered primly. "Watch your step big brother."

The rest of them congratulated her while Benji handed her the water bottle she'd brought with her, then rubbed her shoulders. All of that only lasted maybe fifteen minutes or so before one of the refs came in.

"Hey, we're presenting trophies for all of the women's divisions. Come on."

With one last kiss on Bradley's cheek, she hurried after the ref. It wasn't the craziest fanfare or the biggest crowd, but that didn't matter to Sophia. What mattered was that she had done it.

She'd always felt so small, so easily defeated when it came to her ex. But now, she'd like to see anyone manhandle her. She wasn't the scared, distrustful little girl that she used to be. She believed in *herself*, and that there was hope for tomorrow.

Sophia wished she could go back in time and take the hand of her younger self, assure her that eventually things would be alright, and she wouldn't always have to live on the edge of the knife. That hope was coming, and it was in the form of her handsome, cowboy protector.

The ref announced her name and handed her a trophy that was hardly bigger than her hand, but people probably wouldn't have guessed that judging by the uproar that came from the Millers. They really were her family. Her home. Her comfort.

And if she and Bradley ever decided to add to that family, she knew their children would feel the same assurance and comfort she did every day.

But first... skydiving lessons. She had a list, after all, and it wasn't going to get itself done.

9

Bryant

here were *so* many babies.

Bryant had been keeping up with his family enough to know that their family reunion was going to have plenty of little ones, but he'd never felt so *surrounded* before. He had to admit, he wasn't exactly big on them, but his hopes that they would keep their distance were looking pretty farfetched.

Sure, they were cute. But Bryant didn't like how demanding they were. And not in a he thought they were selfish kind of way, but in a he was pretty sure he'd somehow mess up and hurt them or scar them for life kind of way. It was fairly anxiety-inducing and made his stomach twist.

"Hey, how's the business going?"

Bryant looked up from his coffee to see Teddy, the wife of one of his cousins. It was kind of weird how the two of them had become friends, but Bryant liked anyone who could fix one of his hotrods while also refraining from proselytizing to him the entire time.

He wasn't the black sheep of the family he had once been. In fact, he tried to swing by the ranch at least once a month. But he still wasn't like his American Pie siblings. He lived in his own place well away from home base, and he still ran his casino and his luxury liquor brand. But he liked to think that he'd done a lot to change his old ways. He'd set up a college fund for underprivileged kids. He'd also started a fund to help low-income youngsters who were struggling with eating disorders. He'd learned from Keiko just how expensive getting a therapist or going to a treatment center could be, and how she was lucky her parents had been able to afford it.

There were other things, of course, but they were smaller. He only drank on special occasions, and never more than a couple at a time. He didn't mess with drugs or party. He tried his best to make the world a little better every day.

"Ah, it's going. Not as much growth as I'd like, but we're trucking along."

Teddy slid across from him, nursing what looked to be a hot chocolate with extra, extra whipped cream. "That's good. Things have been kinda rough lately. Business has fallen off at my pop's place."

"Really?"

She shrugged. "Yeah, but it'll pick up. People will always need car repairs."

"That's true." He rubbed his chin, running through his car collection in his mind. He'd donated and sold about half of them, realizing that he didn't need twenty cars in a garage he rarely visited, so sometimes the details of what he had left were blurry. "I think I have a couple that need tune-ups and whatnot."

"Well bring them over whenever you want! Although I know it's a long drive to Texas."

"Eh, I'll probably just hire a couple of people to drive 'em down there."

Teddy shook her head, a wry smile on her features. "I'm still not used to how y'all have money to do literally whatever you want."

"It's an interesting sort of life," Bryant agreed, wincing as a toddler came running by with their diaper proudly waving from their hand, Chastity running frantically after them. Neither he nor Teddy said anything for a moment, watching with wide eyes.

"There's, uh, a lot of young ones here," Teddy remarked, resting her chin in her hands.

"There sure are."

At that point Keiko returned, holding a piece of Ma Miller's red velvet cake and a steaming cup of coffee. Bryant didn't say anything, but he was happy to see her grabbing a generous slice.

Much like him, Keiko had grown plenty too. She hadn't had a relapse of her eating disorder in over a year and was doing very well at getting at least two meals into her a day without obsessing over calorie counts. Her OCD was also much more in control, and what episodes she did have were fewer and farther apart.

It made him feel so *good* to watch her heal and build coping mechanisms that would help her when times were rough. Keiko deserved peace with her body, peace with her mind, and he worked as hard as he could to make sure she had whatever resources she needed.

"It's at the point where I feel like I'm one of the odd ones out for not having any," Teddy continued. "Seems like it's kinda expected at this point."

"What are we talking about?" Keiko asked, settling in next to Bryant and leaning into his side.

"Ah, just the pressure to get pregnant and have lots of kids," Teddy answered unabashedly. Maybe one of the reasons she and Bryant got along so well was because she was a pretty blunt person.

"Oh," Keiko murmured quizzically before biting into her cake.

"Like, I'm not opposed to them," Teddy said. "I just got stuff I wanna do with the shop, especially with Andre retiring soon."

"Yeah, kids are a lot," Bryant agreed.

Sure, sometimes he felt like he was an odd one out for not even trying for any kids, but mostly he was used to taking a different path than the rest of his family. Besides, he was looking forward to when the plethora of Miller spawn were old enough to recognize him for what he was, which was clearly "the cool uncle." Unfortunately, babies didn't really care about him rolling up with all sorts of cool things and stories, which was clearly a character flaw on their part.

But then Silas and Sterling joined their table, and the conversation drifted from children. A lot had happened all across their family so there was certainly plenty to talk about. From new business endeavors to injuries, to house construction and beyond. At least there were no deaths. Things had certainly been worrisome after Cass' accident several years back, but nothing that harrowing since.

Like most reunions, the celebration, food, and chatter went well into the night. Normally Keiko liked to observe a very specific bedtime as a way to maintain her mental health, but she hadn't asked to go until it was nearly eleven.

But as he drove her to her apartment in town, he could tell that something was wrong. Her mood was... just a hair off. Not enough that he would say she was outright upset, but he'd long since learned how to tell when her mood was going south.

"Hey, you alright?" he asked as he pulled up to her apartment. She'd moved since he'd first met her, into a much bigger place that was closer to the edge of town. But once her lease was up, she and Bryant were supposed to finally marry and move into a house a couple of miles from the rest of the family. It was enough space that Bryant wouldn't feel smothered, but it wouldn't isolate Keiko from her support system.

She didn't answer for a moment, looking out of the window and staring into the dark of the night. Bryant didn't rush her, knowing that sometimes she just needed to think about things. But as the seconds turned into minutes, he started to feel more and more concerned.

But eventually, she did speak, her voice barely more than a whisper.

"I... there were a lot of children around today."

"Yeah, Teddy and I pointed that out earlier."

"I remember." She clammed up again, but Bryant knew he just had to wait her out. Let her think. It wasn't exactly easy, but it was something he needed to do for her. "We're supposed to be married soon."

"Yes, we are."

Another long, choking silence. Bryant put the car into park, knowing that bouncing his foot on the break in anticipation wouldn't help either of them.

"Even after we're married, I don't want to have children. I might not ever want to have children."

"Keiko, why are you bringing this up now?"

"I just... I wanted to make sure we had the right expectations. I didn't want you to think that I would be willing to just grow your family in that way."

Bryant could hear the self-consciousness in her voice, and it made his heart ache. Keiko had grown so much, but there were still certain things that could set her off. Sometimes they were serious issues. Sometimes it was just that mean little voice in the back of her head that told her that she was too broken for him to love.

Carefully, he reached over and took her hand in his. He waited until she looked at him, really looked at him, before it was his turn to speak.

"Keiko, I love you, and only you. We've been waiting a long time to get married because you and I needed a long time. So I would never dream of trying to rush you into having children."

"Really?"

"Yes. And besides, I'm not even sure that I want to have kids. They're a whole lot of responsibility that I'm not sure I'm ready for. And like you said, I don't know if I ever will be. My parents had a lot of kids, sure, but I think that was to my detriment. And Benji's too."

Keiko let out a long, long breath, almost slumping in her seat.

"Thank you, Bryant. That means a lot to me."

"Of course, Keiko. I promised myself to you, and that means we do things our way. Just the two of us."

"Just the two of us," she agreed, leaning in to give him a kiss. "I love you."

"I love you too. From the bottom of my heart."

And he meant it. Wherever their paths led, he was fine as long as it was with Keiko.

10

Keiko

Keiko heard the familiar sound of her letter box's lid opening, then closing, and practically sprinted out of her apartment.

Please be here, please be here, please be here!

"Whoa, where are you going in a hurry?" Bryant asked, looking up from his work laptop. It wasn't often that he got the time to stay for an entire weekend, but he'd found that he was able to do it more often when he brought a means of doing at least some cursory work.

"Mail's here!" Keiko called, throwing on her hall slippers and bursting out of the door.

"Why are you—oh, right."

She reached the mailbox in seconds flat, but she paused right before opening it, her hands shaking slightly.

She'd been basically stalking her mail for the past week and a half, hoping that every day was *the* day. But the more time that went without an answer, the more she began to doubt she would ever get one at all.

Patience wasn't really her strong suit, and after mailing out her manuscript for her book on both OCD and her eating disorder over a month ago, her nerves were growing increasingly frayed.

"This is it," Keiko told herself, taking a deep breath. "I'm manifesting my success."

She felt a bit silly saying it, but it was one of the things her therapist was having her try out. Instead of constantly focusing on the negative, she put that energy into envisioning positive things happening instead.

"Hey, you okay?" Bryant asked, sticking his head out of the doorway.

"Yeah, I'm alright," Keiko said, steeling herself before reaching in. Sure enough, there were three letters in there, and she grabbed them. "Let's head inside."

Bryant nodded, letting her past. "Anything good?"

She didn't answer right away, carding through them. The first was a utilities bill. The second was her internet bill.

But then there it was, finally, a letter from one of the literary agencies she had sent a query to.

"Oh my gosh!" she gasped, holding it in quivering hands. "It's here! It's actually here!"

"Ya gonna open it?"

"No, I thought I would sit here a while and just admire the envelope," she shot back, giving Bryant a rueful look.

"Right, right. Point taken. I just can't believe it's here."

"Me either."

But Keiko did love Bryant's enthusiasm. He'd offered to fund the publication of her book, but Keiko wanted to go about it the traditional way. She knew a lot of people would kill to have the resources she did through Bryant, but it was something she needed to do on her own. Months and months of work, research, and time had gone into the whole project, and she couldn't believe that the fruition of it all was right in her hands.

Taking another deep breath, Keiko finally opened the letter, tearing off the flap and quickly unfolding the paper. Her eyes shuttled across it as fast as she'd read in ages, adrenaline pumping through her system.

"Well, what is it? What did they say?"

Keiko didn't answer, pouring over the words.

"Keiko?"

And then she got to it. The sentence that she'd been afraid of.

"They've decided to pass on my manuscript," Keiko whispered, setting the letter down on her coffee table. She could clean it up later.

"Oh, Keiko, I'm so sorry."

"It's alright. I knew that the chances of being rejected were way higher than the chances of being accepted. Most authors get at least five of them before they ever get approved."

But still, even though she knew that, she had hoped. And now that hope was sinking into a deep, dark pit inside of her.

"Hey, you okay there?"

Bryant took her into his arms, gently pulling her flush to his chest. Keiko let herself lean against him, closing her eyes against the flood of bad feelings going through her. Breathe in. Breathe out. She just needed to get over the initial shock of disappointment and it would be fine.

"You're gonna get there, Keiko. I know you are. And I'll always be by your side, rooting for you the entire way."

"Thank you, Bryant. And I'll be fine, I promise. But maybe today is a biscuits and gravy kind of day."

"Sounds good. Want me to order some?"

"Do you think Ma Miller has any cooked up? No one else's really compares."

"Hah! I'm sure if I called her up, she'd be happy to make some. Probably even get one of my brothers to deliver if you don't feel up to visiting."

"No, I think I'd like to visit. Let's just not tell them about the rejection letter. At least not yet."

"That's fair. Why don't you take a shower and get out of your pajamas while I call Ma?"

Keiko nodded, heading to the bathroom to do just that. She spent much longer under the water than she normally would have, the heated stream helping to wash away many of the negative feelings that were building up inside her. Just like she'd said, as the minutes ticked by, the shock of the whole situation began to fade.

It was alright. She had sent off four different query letters on her first round, and she had a b-list in case all of those rejected her. She hadn't reached the end of her journey, just a little pit stop along the path.

By the time she was out of the shower, dried, and dressed, she was almost back to normal, if not a little melancholy around the edges.

"What did your mother say?" she asked, seeing Bryant was back at his laptop again.

"She's already on it and looking forward to seeing us," he

answered with a smile, typing a couple more things before closing his computer. "You ready to go?"

"Yeah, let me just get my shoes on."

"Right, that's probably important."

Keiko crooked a smile at that, heading over to her shoe rack to pick some comfortable flats. But as she looked over her selection, a knock sounded at her door.

"Are you expecting anyone?"

"No, not really," she answered, crossing to her peephole. "It's the mailman!"

"Didn't he already swing by?"

He had, so it was pretty unusual for him to be there again. But hope flickered back to life in her chest and she cautiously opened the door.

"Yes?"

"Hey, sorry to bother you, but I noticed a letter for your house got stuck in one of the seams at the bottom of my bag. It looked pretty important, so I wanted to make sure I circled 'round and gave it to you."

Keiko stared at him with wide eyes, trying not to hope too hard. "Oh, thank you. That's so kind of you."

"Just doin' my job, ma'am. You have a good day!"

He walked off, leaving the letter in her *once again* trembling hands. Keiko couldn't bring herself to look down for a moment, not until Bryant came over.

"What's going on?"

"I had a letter stuck in his bag," Keiko murmured, stepping back inside and closing the door.

"Oh, is it from…?"

"I don't know."

Half numb, half about to explode out of her own skin, Keiko crossed to her couch and sat down. Finally, once she was sure that her feet wouldn't go out from under her, she looked at the envelope.

"It's from a different literary agency."

Bryant was beside her in nearly an instant. "Do you want to wait until after we come back from Ma's to open it?"

Keiko thought about it, weighing the pros and cons rapidly in her head. "I... I think I'm gonna open it now. I think I'll be too distracted by anticipation if I try to leave without knowing."

"Fair enough. I'm right here beside you."

Yes, he was indeed. And she had no doubt of that at all. And maybe it was that certainty that allowed her to rip open the envelope and pull the letter out without any hesitation. Just like the first one, she read it at a ravenous pace, devouring the words as fast as her brain could comprehend them. This time, however, Bryant stayed quiet until the letter tumbled from her hand.

"Keiko, I'm so sorry—"

"They want to represent my manuscript."

"Wait, what?"

She jumped to her feet, full of so much emotion again that she was worried it would burst out from her core like a supernova. "They accepted me! They want to represent my manuscript to different publishing houses!"

"Keiko, that's amazing!"

"It is!"

Suddenly she was in his arms, and he was whirling her around, both of them laughing and crying with elation. She couldn't believe it. After that first letter, she was sure she was in for the long haul with needing to go through multiple rounds of rejections. But no, she'd only had to wait an hour or two. What were the chances!?

"Man, Ma is gonna be so thrilled to hear this!"

"I can't wait to tell her!" Keiko agreed, wiping happy tears from her face. "I can't wait to tell *everyone!*"

"I knew you could do it, Keiko. You have a real gift. Your book is gonna help a lot of people, I think."

Keiko shut her eyes against the deluge of everything. Pride, relief, joy, it all mixed together within her. When she was younger, there hadn't exactly been a ton of resources for what she was going through. And what few that she could get her hands on were always so clinical and detached. She hoped that if there were other girls and boys going through the same thing, they would find her book and see themselves in it. It was part love letter, part advice, part hope for the future. A future she'd always thought she never could have because of her broken self-worth.

"I couldn't have done this without you," she whispered, throwing her arms around his shoulders and holding tightly. "Thank you, Bryant."

"Nah, you would have found the path without me. But I sure am glad that I'm here to watch you kick butt on it."

Keiko grinned, kissing all over his face until she dissolved into happy giggles. She couldn't believe it. She really couldn't. She was going to be a published author! Or at least she would once her literary agent found a publishing house to represent her.

Amazing.

"Come on," she said, feeling like she could float right out the door. "Ma is waiting."

"That she is. I hope you're gonna want cake later, because this is definitely gonna be a cake-worthy announcement for her."

"Bring it on," Keiko said, gripping his hands. She felt like she could conquer anything, and she was going to ride that feeling as long as it lasted. "Today is certainly worthy of celebration."

"That's my girl."

PART II

MILLER BROTHERS OF TEXAS WRAP-UP

11

Samuel

"*P*eekaboo!"

There was nothing quite like the giggle of a baby. Samuel could listen to it all day, which was probably why he was the second-best peekaboo master at the Montana Millers household. The only one to beat him out was Ben, if only because his kids were school-aged, so he had time away from them which he was more than happy to loan out for babysitting duties.

"Peekaboo!"

"Goodness," Ma Miller said, coming up behind him in one of the upstairs bedrooms and handing him an iced tea as well as a sippy cup for Dani and Benji's newest baby. She was a chunky little thing, all giggles and big eyes in all the best ways.

They'd had a bumper crop of pregnancies last summer and

fall, with Chastity and Dani both expecting, but the real surprise had been him and Ginny finally throwing their hat into the race.

They hadn't been avoiding having babies, per se, but there was a lot that Ginny wanted to do before and after they got married. Plus, she'd have to stop with her self-defense classes and MMA for at least a year, which Samuel understood why she wouldn't want to do that. She and Missy had both worked really hard to have a steady group of students they taught in town, and he could tell Ginny was proud of her work.

But then she'd missed her period.

It hadn't been intentional, but they took it as a sign that it was time to start, and that's how little Caspian had made his announcement. He was an onery little guy—that was for sure—and Ginny had had the worst morning sickness almost her entire pregnancy. Along with fatigue. And persistent headaches. Samuel was there with her the entire time, obviously, but there was only so much he could do for her when it was their son inside of her that was giving her grief.

Clearly, Caspian took after his mother, because he insisted on arriving early. There weren't many severe complications, but there were enough that he was scheduled to spend an entire month in the NICU. They were about three weeks through it, and Samuel was itching for their boy to come home.

It was hard, being separated from Caspian. The first week, he and Ginny lived at the hospital. But then the doctors had told them that it would be better for all of them if they went some-where to get some real rest, especially Ginny, who would want to truly recuperate before their son was home full time. So they decided to get a hotel room not too far from the hospital. And Samuel made it back to the ranch a few different times to get them fresh clothes to wear. It had been difficult to leave, but the doctor had been right, and the next week the two of them had visited every day for several hours.

Today, however, was one of the days Ginny asked to be left there alone for most of the day. She didn't ask it often, but Samuel understood that sometimes she just wanted to sit in the quiet and bottle feed their son, maybe even nap beside him. Samuel would have been there in a moment if she needed him, but he understood that sometimes, he did more for her by taking care of their home than sitting staring at her and their son in the hospital.

"Ow!" was the only warning he had before a loud wail filled the house.

"Oh goodness. I just left him alone for a second!" Ma Miller said.

"Here, watch the baby," Samuel said, already on his feet and vaulting down the stairs toward the kitchen. Like every parent, about a dozen and one worst-case scenarios played through his head. Thankfully, he didn't come across a bloodbath, but instead Ben's little guy was holding his red finger up, the nail already beginning to bruise.

"Hey, buddy, what happened here?"

"Gramma wanted to make lemonade, so I was trying to help her get the squeezer, but then the drawer closed on my finger!" The shock of the moment seemed to be fading from the boy, and he stopped wailing to let out a few sniffles. "I'm sorry I made a ruckus. Am I gonna lose my nail?"

What a sweet kid. He'd just started kindergarten, or maybe first grade if Samuel remembered right. It figured he'd gotten hurt while trying to help out.

"Aw, maybe buddy, but it'll grow back. You want me to get some ice for you and maybe some medicine?"

"They got medicine for nails?"

"Well, not for the nail, but to help with the swelling and pain."

"Oh, okay. Thank you, Uncle Samuel."

"No problem, buddy. Let me just tell your Gramma that everything's alright, okay? You gave us both a scare."

"Sorry. I make lemonade all the time at home. I just forgot the drawers here do the slidey thing."

"The slidey thing?"

"Yeah, they go back in on their own."

Oh, right. Samuel tended to forget about that too. But since Ma Miller was getting on in age and had lots of children around, she'd had Pa install some sort of spring load that gently slid all of the cabinets shut.

"Why don't you settle in the living room and put something on the TV while I get all that for you? You got a drink you want?"

"Well... I kinda wanted lemonade."

"Hah, right. How about some water to take your medicine, then I'll get you that lemonade as soon as it's ready?"

"Okay," he murmured, unable to hide his crestfallen expression. "But I really wanted to help."

"I know you did. But accidents happen. The important thing is learning to roll with the punches and take care of yourself."

The boy nodded resolutely and wandered to the living room. Samuel watched him go before grabbing everything he said he would and delivering it to his nephew. After a beat, Samuel asked if there was a movie he wanted to watch, then put it on, draping one of the throw blankets over the kid.

"Thanks, Uncle Samuel. But... can you not tell my daddy?"

Samuel paused at that. "Why not, buddy?"

"I don't want him to think I can't do big boy things. He does *everything.*"

Oh, bless this dear child's heart.

Samuel knew a teaching moment when he heard one, so he sat down next to his l'il nephew. "Listen here. I know your dad is the head of the ranch here since Papa Miller retired, but trust me, he messes up plenty."

"Nooo, that's not true."

"Oh, it most certainly is. But the important thing is he learns, picks himself up, and keeps going. And you know what?"

"What?"

"When your Daddy sees your fingernail, he's not going to think that you messed up. He's just gonna see that you're hurt and be concerned for his boy."

"You think so?"

"I know so. I've been working on his crew for quite a few years, and I gotta say I ain't never seen him call anyone names. Especially not someone he loves so much like you."

The kid nodded resolutely, seemingly feeling much better, then returned his attention to the TV. Once Samuel was sure the matter was over, he went to the kitchen to finish up that lemonade that started everything.

But as he squeezed the lemons, got the sugar, and did everything else, Samuel couldn't help but notice that his gut was twisting hard. He couldn't quite put a finger on why, other than leftover adrenaline from hearing the kid cry out.

"There you are. I trust it all turned out alright?"

Samuel turned to see Ma Miller standing in the doorway of the kitchen, looking amused. "Yeah. Poor kid got his finger pinched in the drawer. Definitely gonna bruise under his nail. Might even lose it in a bit."

"Poor thing. But I'm glad it wasn't anything too serious."

"Me too."

There was a lull as Samuel kept on squeezing lemons, but he should have known he couldn't slip one past the wise woman.

"What's wrong?"

Samuel paused, feeling his cheeks color a bit. "What do you mean?"

"I can tell that something's bothering you."

Sighing, Samuel set the lemons down and tried to collect himself. "I can't tell you, to be honest. I feel—I don't know, agitated maybe? On edge? And I'm not sure why."

"I think I know, my dear," Mrs. Miller said, her voice all soft and full of understanding.

"Ya mind enlightening me? Because this is pretty uncomfortable."

She paused a moment to coo at the baby in her arms before handing the little girl over to Samuel and taking over the lemonade duties. "Is it possible, you think, that with everything going on with your own son, seeing a little one get hurt might stir up a lot of emotions in you?

"You know Caspian will be alright, but it's been a hard month. And next week he'll be living full time with you, which no doubt is bringing up a lot of protective emotions."

Samuel sat there a moment, looking down at the beautiful baby in his arms as he thought.

"I guess I never put it in that perspective."

But it made sense. That twisting ball in his gut wasn't just adrenaline. It was anxiety. His boy, his precious, beautiful boy, was going to get hurt someday. He'd fall, as children often did. He'd pinch his fingers in drawers. All of those were normal things, and yet any time Samuel thought about it, he just saw hospital wires, oxygen masks, and the little pod-like bed his son had slept in for the past three weeks.

It was a lot.

But Ma Miller just rested her head against his arm for a moment, a comforting touch. "I know it's scary, especially since you've had a bit of a rough start. But you're here with family, Sammy. We're all gonna take care of each other."

And that was true. Hadn't he just helped out Ben's kid? And he and Ma Miller were both watching Benji's baby girl. Without a doubt he knew that their kid would have a literal army of aunts, uncles, and cousins to help him through.

No one was ever abandoned on the Miller Ranch. And he quite liked that.

"Just one more week," he said with a nod, that anxiety ball simmering down.

"Atta boy, Sammy. Just remember to cherish the time and the people you have around you. It always goes so fast."

12

Ginny

*U*gh.

Ginny looked at herself in the mirror, for once in a rare moment of solitude. She'd been avoiding the reflective surfaces lately, but for some reason, she'd decided to stop and take a peek.

Bad idea.

"What happened..." she breathed to herself as she looked at a reflection that didn't feel like her. Although she knew exactly what happened. It'd been six months since her pregnancy, and she'd felt pretty gross the entire time.

Not that she didn't love her little prince, Caspian. No, he was the bright and shining point that got her through most days. Well, him and Samuel. But even her beautiful baby boy couldn't fix just how *gross* she felt.

Thankfully her mastitis had finally cleared up, which was a huge relief, but it left her feeling somewhat betrayed by her own body. She had a baby, then she was supposed to make milk. Easy peasy. But no, she had to go off and deliver early, then two months out of the hospital get a terrible infection.

It wasn't just that either. She hadn't washed her hair in a week; she had baby vomit on her shirt. She was beginning to break out around her period again, which was something she thought she left behind in high school.

The skin on her stomach was still a bit droopy and puckered. The bags under her eyes would be considered too large to be a carry-on if she tried to go flying, and her energy levels were... nonexistent.

Yeah, it wasn't going well for Ginny. Not at all.

"Come on, girl—pull yourself together," she whispered to herself. But then Caspian let out a cry from his crib a few feet away and she hurried to check in on him.

It must have just been a bad dream or momentary discomfort, because he stopped almost the moment she leaned over to check on him, smiling sleepily before his eyelids slid closed.

"That's my boy. You stay nice and cozy."

The worst part though was that Ginny felt ungrateful and selfish for complaining, so she just didn't. After all, since marrying Samuel she'd basically become richer than she could have ever imagined. She could buy or have whatever she wanted. She had amazing medical insurance. She had so many people offering to hang out with her or do chores that she could just sit on her rear and let them clean her entire house.

How many people could say they had all that? Not many. So even though she felt pretty miserable, she was fairly certain she'd feel worse if she complained. Instead, she just tucked her head down and tried to keep on top of things.

And avoid reflective surfaces.

A gentle knock on the door interrupted her critical gaze at her reflection, and Ginny hurried downstairs. Opening it, she was surprised to see Ma Miller standing there.

"Oh, Benji's out right now."

"That's alright, dear. I actually came over to help watch little Caspian for you."

"Oh?" While Ma Miller had definitely watched him several times while Ginny was recovering, that'd always been at the main house. Ginny had figured it was easier for the older woman to be in the place most familiar to her, considering her eyesight was just beginning to go and so were her knees. "Do you want me to cart him over?"

"No, no, I'll be just fine watching him here. I'll just go get myself up to his nursey room."

She tottered past, all smiles, and then to Ginny's surprise, Samuel popped out from the side of the doorway.

Ginny jumped back, heart racing. "Holy halibut on a stick! You startled me!"

"Awww, sorry about that, darling. But why don't you get changed into something clean and comfortable so I can make it up to you?"

Ginny eyed him suspiciously. Samuel wasn't a guy for a lot of pomp and circumstance, but he did have a romantic streak about a mile wide. Ginny loved that about him—she did—but she wasn't sure she wanted to be romanced right now.

"I need to shower."

"That's perfectly alright. How about I brew us up some coffee while you go 'bout all that?"

Ginny eyed him suspiciously. Something was definitely up. But with Ma Miller agreeing to watch Caspian and her husband around as backup, there was no way she could resist taking as long a shower as she wanted.

"Alright. Give me like, half an hour."

"Take as long as you want, love. I'll always be here."

It was an off-handed comment, but it struck Ginny just right and she felt a surge of emotion rush through her. But she didn't want to burst into tears right then and there, so she hurried up to get washed.

A little over a half hour later, she headed down the stairs only to have Samuel press a travel mug of steaming hot coffee into her hand.

"Bless you," she said, taking a deep whiff.

"Anything for you."

Goodness, he was really laying it on thick. Had he done something wrong and was trying to make up for it? Well, the joke was on him because Ginny didn't really have any idea of what was going on outside of her son and their day-to-day existence. She loved being a mother—she did—but no one had told her that her entire life was going to become so much smaller in a way. Her martial arts was on hold for a while until her body recovered, as was her work. Even her gym routine. Not that she ever really went to the gym, much preferring to get her workouts done on the farm.

"You ready to head out?"

"Are you gonna tell me where we're going?"

"Nope."

"And it's okay that I'm going there in sweats?" At the beginning of her pregnancy, Ginny had tried to buy at least a couple of cute maternity outfits. But once she was halfway through her second trimester, things had gotten a whole lot harder and she pretty much gave up on ever looking stylish.

"Yup."

Ginny narrowed her eyes at him again, but he just kept grinning blithely. Clearly, he was up to something, but what?

"I've got my eye on you, Samuel."

"And I wouldn't have it any other way."

He held out his hand and Ginny took it, letting him lead her out to his truck. She did have to admit, the farther she got from the house, the more it sank in that she was actually going to get to kick back and relax. What a novel idea.

She thought that she'd be anxious to be away from her little one, but she knew Caspian was in good hands with Ma Miller. She didn't have to worry about the little guy at all. And that was nice. Real nice.

So by the time they reached the city, Ginny was doing her all not to bounce in her seat. She still felt tired, but she *didn't* feel nearly as gross or inhuman anymore.

"Would you like to stop and get that funny tea you and Dani are obsessed with?"

Ginny gasped and whirled in her seat to face her husband. "Do you mean *boba!?*"

He chuckled lightly. "Yeah, I guess that's what I mean. The one with the flavor balls in it."

She nodded eagerly, grinning broadly. "Oh boy, yes, I want some boba. Are we going to the fancy place in uptown?"

"Yeah, I remember you liked that one quite a lot."

Ginny clapped her hands, no longer resisting the urge to bounce in her seat. "Oh man, I don't think I've had that since..."

"Since our little guy was born. It was one of the first things I got you once you were allowed to eat."

Oh, that was right. The entire week right after Caspian was born was still pretty blurry in her mind. Sometimes memories would float to the surface, but most of the time it was just a colored blur of vague images.

The boba place was still a good bit away from the exit, so Ginny did her best not to vibrate through the truck's floor. When they finally did arrive, she practically flew out the passenger-side door to get inside.

Thankfully, there wasn't a long line, so all Ginny had to wait for was Samuel to catch up with her before she ordered. And if she just so happened to pick out five different mini cups so she could have all her favorite flavors, well... that was her business.

And Samuel, the amazing man that he was, just sat across from her sipping at his black tea while she methodically worked her way through hers. By the time she finished, she was feeling very full of liquid but quite content.

"Thank you for doing this," she said as Samuel led her back to their truck, his arms looped through hers.

"Oh, we're not done yet."

"We're not?" What else could he do? Sure, there were plenty of options if everything were normal, but much fewer options where sweatpants were appropriate.

"Nope."

Ah, he was back to monosyllabic answers. Great.

Nevertheless, Ginny got back into the truck. Considering how great the Boba surprise had been, she was fairly certain that he had something great up his flannel sleeves.

She didn't quite recognize where they were going, but she did know they were going somewhere in the more expensive side of the city as they drove wherever it was that Samuel was taking her. Her leg bounced, and after fifteen minutes or so, her bladder began to complain about just how much boba she drank.

"Is it that much farther? Cause I might blow any second now."

"Just another minute or so."

And true to his word, they rounded a corner and he pulled up to a place she didn't recognize at all. It wasn't until she was out of the truck that she realized it was a high-end spa.

"Wait, is this it?" she asked, pointing in shock.

He nodded. "Figured you could use a little pampering. I booked just about all you could get in a single day in there, so why don't you go enjoy?"

"What about you?"

"Ah, I scheduled us a couple's massage with aromatherapy and hot stones, but that won't be until later. I'll be around though. Don't you worry."

Ginny nodded and hustled in, visiting the restroom first before actually starting her relaxation journey. It was so easy to forget that she had money now and could treat herself in ways that she never could hope to before. Thankfully, she had Samuel to spoil her.

And she certainly felt spoiled. She got a steam treatment, then a facial. She had their hour and a half couple's massage with all the fixings. She got her brows shaped, her nails done, and even a pedicure. Even the time between treatments was relaxing. They had her sit in an oversized, fluffy bathrobe with flutes of champagne or bubbly water and strawberries around on chilled platters. Ginny didn't drink much, she'd kind of developed an aversion to the smell of most alcohol when she got pregnant, but she enjoyed a couple of flavored bubbly waters while feeling fancy and spoiled.

It was late by the time everything wrapped up, and Ginny was pretty certain that she was floating on a cloud instead of physically walking.

"That was *wonderful*," she said to Samuel as he pulled up in the truck and helped her inside. She knew her face was a little red and raw from her facial, and the area around her brows stung a little bit, but it was a pleasant sort of sensation that reminded her of her younger days. Not that she'd ever been super into spa days with the girls, but there had been a few ladies' nights in her early twenties.

"I'm glad you liked it. Are you feeling a little better?"

Ginny nodded, snuggling up to his side as much as she could considering he was beginning to drive. "I feel more like me," she said. And she meant it. So much of her life as of late had been dedicated to little Caspian that she'd almost felt like she was outside of her own body. Disconnected from Virginia and everything she was meant to be.

But now? Now she felt more connected to herself and less like a baby milk-making machine. She was Ginny Miller, a resilient woman with one heck of a left hook.

"I'm glad. Because you're the most beautiful, amazing woman I've ever met, and even more so, you're the best mom our son could ask for. You deserve to have a day for yourself."

Even after all their years together, Ginny felt herself flush. At least she could mostly blame it on her sensitive cheeks from her facial. "D'awww. You don't have to butter me up after everything else you've done today."

"I'm not buttering you up. I know things haven't been the easiest lately, and it's easy to forget ourselves in the rush of everything. But it's important to me that you know how incredible you are, and that you deserve nice things."

Was he trying to make her cry? It seemed like it, because her eyes were already beginning to water. "Samuel, I love you so much."

"And I love you too, Ginny. Not just as the mother of my child, but as you, yourself. I'm sorry that I let things get hectic, but I never want you to feel overwhelmed or like you can't vent."

Ginny nodded, her voice thick in her throat. "Thank you, Sam. You don't know how much that means to me."

"Well, you have no idea how much *you* mean to me."

Ginny resolved to kiss him stupid the moment they were out of the truck, but for the moment, she just leaned against him and let her eyes flutter closed. She was having a *great* day, and she resolved to make sure she didn't wait so long before her next one.

13

Solomon

"Is it just me, or are there more kids here than ever?"

Solomon looked to his cousin, Bryant, and gave an idle sort of nod. "I reckon you're right."

There *were* a *lot* of kids at the most recent family reunion. Granted, there'd been a lot of kids at the last one, but the Millers up north kept right on reproducing, apparently. Somehow, although they'd been together the shortest out of the McLintoc Millers, Simon and Leilani were the only couple to have a kid so far. Mom was trying not to hound them about grandbabies, but Solomon could tell that she was a wee bit jealous of her sister-in-law up north with her bevy of young ones to spoil.

"Hey, do y'all have any headache meds?" Silas said, wandering up with a concerned expression on his face.

But Bryant shook his head. "I'm not sure, but I can go ask Ma. Something up?"

"Teddy has a bad headache, maybe even a migraine. I want to get some meds in her, then put her to bed."

Solomon let out a small chuckle, which made his little brother shoot him a look. "Sorry, just the idea of you putting her to bed is kind of funny. Given, ya know, how she is."

"Driven to a fault and willing to put her physical needs aside more often than not?"

"Yup. Exactly."

Silas let out a sigh. "This is about the only time she'd ever allow me to mother her. But yeah, Bryant, if you could go ask, that'd be a godsend."

"Walk with me. We'll find out together."

The two left and Solomon was once again alone with his thoughts. He watched the children, some running around, some sitting down to snack, but all of them were so full of life. Was he ever that young? It felt like ages ago, if he was being honest.

But he should have known not to maintain eye contact for so long, because two of the older ones ran over to him.

"Uncle Solomon! Come play with us!"

They grabbed his hands, theirs so much smaller than his, and pulled him to his feet. Solomon could have told them no, but he had a big heart so that wasn't really possible.

"What are we playing?"

"Red light–green light! You be the caller!"

Now that was something he could handle. "Okay then. Now no cheating, right? You're not gonna push each other or try to sneak in my peripherals?"

"What's a perry furals?" the girl, Ginger, asked.

"Eh, don't worry about it. It's not important."

"Okay!"

And just like kids did, they let it go and herded him over to a tree and told him to close his eyes. It was far more charming than it had any right to be, and he did as he was asked.

Sure, Solomon never thought he'd spend an hour or so in his thirties playing red light–green light, but at least they weren't asking him to ref Red Rover. That game always ended up with someone accusing someone else of cheating.

They ended up going all the way until Auntie Miller brought out the cake, which naturally almost all of the kids rushed towards. Released from his duties, Solomon scanned the crowd for Frenchie.

He saw her long before she saw him, his wife deep in conversation with Dani. She was talking with her hands, as usual, her teal hair piled on top of her head. It wasn't his favorite color on her—that had to be her natural deep brown—but he was happy that she finally had the resources to do whatever she wanted with her hair. Not too long into their dating, she'd revealed that she'd been cutting it herself since she was young. It had taken him a surprisingly long time to convince the stubborn young woman to let him take her to a high-end salon, but she'd begrudgingly admitted that it was a pretty nice experience. She still tended to dye her hair and do trims herself, but once or twice a year she'd let herself completely be pampered, and that was much better than nothing in Solomon's opinion.

Of course, if he had his way, Francesca would spend every day spoiled, pampered, and wrapped up in the softest, finest things. He thought that after so long together his compulsion to take care of her might ebb a little, but the more he fell in love with her, the more that instinct grew.

But now, as he looked at her broad smile, her frame that had finally filled in a little after several years of good eating, those hands that gestured everywhere, the more he began to think. And the more he began to think, the more he couldn't help but wonder if it would be nice to start a family of their own.

It wasn't the most preposterous idea. Not at all. After all, they were married and had been for over a year. Then again, like with most things, Frenchie liked to move slow with their relationship. They'd been engaged nearly last in his set of brothers despite dating first. Their marriage fell somewhere in the middle.

Not that Solomon minded. No. Not one drop. He wanted Frenchie to take her time and never feel forced into anything again. And it made him feel strangely proud, in a way. Frenchie had a lot of trust issues, especially when it came to men, but she chose to trust *him*. Despite all that paranoia and experience in her telling herself that he was dangerous, she chose to love him, to be with him, to spend the rest of their lives together.

So if she needed an extra year to prepare for certain life events, the least Solomon could do was support her in that.

But still... he imagined a little one with her eyes and smile but his hair, bouncing on her knee while he worked with a farrier to learn how to properly reshoe his horse. He thought of putting a band-aid on their daughter's knee after falling from her bike. He thought of birthdays and Christmasses and Frenchie reading them bedtime stories a bit later at night than they should be up.

And he fell in love with those imaginings. Enough to resolve himself to talk to her about it. But later, maybe. At a family reunion probably wasn't the best time to tell her he was interested in having a baby. Or maybe it was, considering all the life and joy around them.

He'd have to wait and see if any of the kids threw up or bit anybody. That would be the real clincher. She'd probably say no anyway. She still had a lot of life she wanted to catch up on that had been denied to her for most of her childhood.

"Hey there, handsome!" Frenchie called, her eyes catching his. "Did you have fun with the horde?"

"Of course," he answered, grinning from ear to ear. "I think I'm working my way up to being one of their favorite uncles."

"Aren't you technically like their cousin once removed or something?" she asked, tilting her head to the side in that curious way of hers.

"I mean, technically I suppose my father is the uncle of their fathers so... yes? Maybe? We might just be plain cousins. But it makes things much easier for them to all just call us their various aunts and uncles."

"I get it. When I think of a cousin, I don't think of a relative that's thirty years older than me."

"Funny, you've never mentioned your cousins before."

"Because I never really knew them much to mention anything. Can't even remember most of their names. My stepfather kept us pretty isolated from my mother's side of the family."

Even though they'd been together for years, and Solomon was pretty sure he'd heard everything about that awful man that he could, his temper still licked up at the mention of the abuser. Occasionally he thought of hiring a PI to find the guy and give him his just desserts, but Frenchie had pleaded with him never to initiate any sort of contact, afraid that the man would somehow infect her life again. So, although he'd give quite a sum to exact a little justice, he respected that his wife's need for emotional security was more important.

It was still tempting though.

"You look like you've got a lot on your mind."

He did, and for a moment he thought about asking her the baby question, but then Missy called Frenchie over, wanting to ask her some interior decorating questions. Solomon let her go, knowing the timing wasn't quite right yet.

But in the meantime, at least he could dream.

14

Frenchie

$\mathcal{F}$renchie paced back and forth in the tiny amount of space she had in the long line of fellow graduates. After years of work, studying, and probably more than her fair share of tears, she was finally graduating from college.

She couldn't believe it. Little Francesca, the street urchin, was going to be a real college graduate with a real degree! She could hardly believe it herself, even dressed up in a cap and gown with about three hundred other graduates waiting with her.

Frenchie was well aware that she could have just rested on her laurels. After all, Solomon had made it clear about a dozen times over that he would take care of whatever she needed, education or not. But something in her wouldn't allow for that. It wasn't that she didn't trust him, or that she was worried he would break his word. No, nothing of the sort. It was just that after being denied even the most basic of things for so long, she wanted to experience everything she'd lost out on.

So, she'd gotten her GED. At the time she'd thought that would be enough and she wouldn't feel as dumb. But then she remembered how forlornly she'd watched the college kids walking about campus, laughing and playing games in the court. It had been a good place to scrounge food from free events and the like until security had learned her face and started chasing her out.

So, she'd gone to a community college. She'd gotten her Associate's degree and had stopped for a year, focusing on some of the outreach programs that were well and thriving in Teddy's community center. But after a year off, she began to long for more.

So, she went back to school and started working on her BA. It wasn't easy, and she switched majors once. But finally, well into her twenties, she was graduating with a BA in Digital Media and a minor in architecture.

She almost wanted to pinch herself but figured that would be somewhat embarrassing considering how surrounded she was by other graduates. It looked like it would just be her pacing. She was going to work herself up into a real tizzy if she didn't get a hold of the rushing emotions in her, but if there ever was a day that justified a little bit of a tizzy, getting her degree was one of them. Frenchie supposed that she could always go on to get her masters, but she was pretty sure that she was officially done. She'd climbed the mountain that she'd wanted to conquer, and she had a lot of other things that she wanted to accomplish.

However, she wasn't going to get any of them done until she got out of the hall that she and the rest of her class were lined up in, waiting for their entrance.

Thankfully she managed not to wear a hole in the floor before their musical cue drifted through the double doors at the end of the hall. Frenchie never thought she'd be the type to tear up at "Pomp and Circumstance," but she was definitely getting misty-eyed.

And finally, after what seemed like forever, they were marching forward.

Technically, Frenchie had seen inside the large commencement hall before, but it was another thing entirely to see it jam-packed full of people. Families, friends, partners, over a thousand people all with their own stories and students to support. It was mind-boggling, that was for certain. But perhaps even more over-whelming was the entire section of seating that was taken up by none other than the Millers.

"Frenchie! Smile!"

That was Mrs. Miller, of course, who had a camera practically pressed right up against her glasses. Mr. Miller was there too, looking only mildly miserable.

Frenchie supposed that in and of itself was a small miracle. It was no secret to anyone that the McLintoc Miller's entire family situation had been a bit rocky since the brothers all staged a coup, but things had been getting slowly better ever since his wife threatened to leave him if he didn't shape up.

He'd started therapy, and he'd started going to a church other than the mega-one that Frenchie had tagged when she first met Solomon. He was doing his best to be a nicer, less acerbic person. He was by no means an angel, or even an enjoyable human to be around, but he was trying and that was what mattered to Frenchie.

But besides the Texas patriarch, there was Solomon, Silas, Sterling, Nova, Elizabeth and Tawny. Leilani and Simon were back in Hawaii again, working on some sort of important protest to protect a native religious site. But Leilani had promised to be there digitally, which made sense why Nova was holding her phone up like a news reporter trying to catch the latest scoop.

"That's my daughter!" Mrs. Miller declared proudly, still snapping away with her camera. Frenchie couldn't help but blush, a warm, syrupy feeling flooding her. Mrs. Miller really was the mother she'd always wanted and never had. Between hours spent in the chicken coop together, or out gardening, or even teaching the older woman how to paint, their bond had been formed slowly but naturally. Frenchie didn't exactly trust easy, but Mrs. Miller had more than won her over.

She still couldn't quite work herself up to calling the woman "Mom" yet, but maybe that would come in time. If not, Frenchie wasn't going to stress about it.

As she slowly marched past the Millers to get to her seat, the rest of the ceremony became a blur. There were speakers, some funny jokes, and a whole lot of clapping, but it all kind of blended together into a happy sort of collage.

Right up until it was her turn to walk across the stage. Suddenly her heart was beating in her chest, and she was more scared and terrified than when she'd tried to take her driver's test the first time. But unlike that, there was no chance of failure. She'd already done it. She'd earned her degree and all she had to do was go over and collect it.

It was such a small space. She'd walked farther than that in the dead of winter during the night with shoes that were falling apart. And yet the length of the stage stretched on before her, long and treacherous.

How funny, to have fought so hard to get as far as she had only to get tripped up right at the end. But she couldn't fail now, not after everything she'd accomplished. It was time to stop being so afraid.

Taking a deep breath, Frenchie strode across the stage. Shoulders straight, she focused on just going forward until she finally reached the man who handed her the degree she'd worked so hard for. The moment it was in her hands, there was a raucous cheer from the crowd. That was her Millers, alright.

Feeling like she didn't know whether she wanted to laugh or cry, Frenchie moved the tassel of her cap to the other side, then gave a big ol' wave. She was sure that Mrs. Miller was snapping pictures with her camera like crazy, so she made sure her grin was big and broad.

And just like that, she'd graduated.

It was difficult not to skip right off the stage, but Frenchie somehow managed. She made it back to her seat without imploding, but once more the rest of the ceremony became a blur. She wanted to see her family; she wanted to see *Solomon*. Although she'd done the degree for herself, to prove that she was more than anyone ever thought she could be, she also loved how proud he looked at her accomplishments. He didn't think she was being silly, even if he was willing to totally provide for her. And he didn't diminish her journey even though he'd earned his degree long ago and had way better grades.

No, sometimes when he looked at her, she felt like he was seeing the best that she could possibly be. And it was amazing just how motivating that was. Whenever it seemed like too much, or Frenchie was struggling so hard that she wanted to give up, she'd think about that look he'd get on his face and that soft tone of voice he'd get. That was usually all she needed to take a deep breath and keep right on going.

But it wasn't like she could vault out of her seat. So she

waited. And waited. Eventually it almost seemed like the admin-
istration was making the ceremony run long as a personal spite
to her. But after an age or two, they wrapped it up and all the
graduates were throwing their caps into the air.

There was a sort of traffic jam of people right after, but as
soon as she could, Frenchie rushed over to where the Millers
obviously were sitting and threw herself into Solomon's arms.

"Hey there, graduate," he said, the expression on his face so
incredibly fond. And Frenchie swore she could have melted right
then and there—not just because her robes were incredibly
warm.

"I did it," she said for about the millionth time before
pressing a kiss to his lips. It was a soft and sweet one, appropriate
for a large crowd and in front of family. But even still, she felt
warmth flood through her. Kissing Solomon was like relief,
excitement, and *home* all wrapped into one action. She felt
incredibly safe, which made an interesting companion to the
desire running through her.

It was strange to think that there had once been a time where
she was so terrified by any sort of intimacy that the thought of
kissing a man would make her blood run cold. But that was
another time, another life. Back when she'd been alone, cold and
hungry all the time.

"You did indeed," Solomon answered once they parted. Naturally there was a bit of a procession as everyone else in their party
gave their own hugs and cheek kisses. Even Mr. Miller came up
and gave her a handshake.

But as soon as all of that was done, they started making their
way towards the exit, which took a considerable amount of time
considering just how many people were crammed into the
commencement hall. Once they were out, the Millers all split up

to their separate cars to drive to the city where they had reservations at a fancy restaurant.

"So, how does it feel?" Solomon asked, a broad grin on his face as he opened the car door for her.

"What?"

"Having your degree and conquering the mountain you've been climbing for years?"

Frenchie let out a long breath. "Amazing. Absolutely amazing."

He leaned over and pressed a kiss to her cheek, and Frenchie couldn't help but feel swept up in everything that was *him*. The handsome set of his jaw, the love he had for her, the wisdom and kindness he showed to everyone around him.

Solomon Miller really had turned her life around, but he didn't treat her like a charity case. Not even remotely. He always acted like *she* was the one benefiting him, and she'd never felt so valued in her entire life.

Finally, l'il street rat Frenchie was a real, functioning member of society with a degree and everything. Maybe she could stop fighting so hard to prove herself and instead could... live a little?

"You okay? You look like you're thinkin' pretty hard."

Frenchie looked at her husband, really looked at him, heart swelling in her chest in all the right ways. She really was lucky, wasn't she? And she had the rest of her life to enjoy and experience things with him.

So why not start experiencing them?

"Let's have a baby."

He sat bolt upright and stared at her like she'd grown another head, but Frenchie didn't let that discourage her.

"I've gotten my GED, my Associate's, and now my Bachelor's. I have a pretty steady flow of commissions, and I'm proud of the community outreach programs we've built these past few years. But now?" She leaned closer to him, pulling his face into her hands. "Now I want to build a life, and a family, with *you*."

She had been maybe a little worried that he would react poorly to the idea. After all, Solomon was just about as practical as they came. But instead, he was looking at her as if she were the sun and moon combined.

"Are you sure?" Goodness, there was so much emotion in his voice! Had he been longing to start up their own little line already? How long had he been waiting? Frenchie had no idea. But once again, it was clear that he'd waited for her to be ready, putting their pace in her hands after so many people in her life had denied her even the most basic decisions.

"Absolutely. I'm ready, Solomon. I want this."

And then he was leaning forward, his lips crashing to hers. It wasn't the sweet, soft kiss that they'd shared earlier. No, it was fire and jubilation, love and desire, everything intense and wonderful about their relationship all brandished into a press of lips.

Frenchie wouldn't have it any other way.

15

Silas

"Ugh."

Silas looked over to Teddy, who was sitting at a table with her head in her hands. Definitely a surprise considering she'd just been laughing and idly chatting with Cici, the youngest of all the Millers, just moments earlier.

"Hey, you okay?"

"I just had a really wicked headache come on," she whispered, not lifting her head to look at them. "It's... it's really bad."

"Is it a migraine?"

"No. At least not yet."

"Do you have any of your headache meds on you?"

"I... I can't remember."

"Here, I'll look."

Silas reached towards the pouch strapped to Teddy's thigh.

His wife hated purses. He'd known that for a long while, but she'd been delighted when he'd bought her a sort of hip-bag thing that could hang from her belt with the bottom having a wide and stretchy enough loop to put her leg through, so it was nice and secure against her leg. She wore it to almost every casual gathering, and normally Silas always felt a beam of pride when she did.

However, that pride was most definitely absent while he rooted around for her non-prescription headache meds. She did have some migraine ones back at the cabin where they were staying, but considering how powerful they were, it was best not to use them unless absolutely necessary.

"I'm not finding them," he muttered, checking again in case he just missed them.

But Teddy groaned, sinking farther onto the table. Silas was pretty sure that all the frolicking kids, talking adults, and intense food smells weren't doing her any favors.

"I think maybe I used the last ones on the trip down here when I started to get super car sick."

"Shoot, I do remember that. I'll go see if I can find some."

"Thank you."

Her words were so miserable sounding that Silas couldn't help but feel terrible. Getting to his feet, he tried to scan around for Auntie Miller or anyone else who would know.

Unfortunately, he didn't spot her or her husband, or even their eldest son, Ben. But he did spot Solomon not too far away, and Frenchie almost always carried a full first aid kit with them whenever she left on a trip. Sleep aids, allergy medicine, pain meds, headache meds, sunscreen, pretty much an entire pharmacy. If anyone knew where something would be, it'd be him.

And, as luck would have it, Solomon wasn't sitting alone.

Their cousin Bryant was with him, the two idly chatting. Although Silas was pretty sure that his cousin didn't live in the main house, he stood a pretty good chance of knowing where the medicine was anyway.

"Hey, do y'all have any headache meds?" Silas asked as soon as he was close enough.

Bryant shrugged, his expression worried. "I'm not sure, but I can go ask Ma. Something up?"

To Silas' surprise, Solomon didn't really respond, his stare far off into the distance. Huh, his eldest brother must have had something pretty serious on his mind.

"Teddy has a bad headache," he explained, trying not to sound panicked. He was pretty sure he mostly succeeded. "Maybe even a migraine. I want to get some meds in her, then put her to bed."

Solomon let out a small chuckle, and Silas shot him a look. Was there something funny about Teddy having a headache? Or did he think it wasn't that serious?

If Silas wasn't stressing, he probably would have realized that wasn't anything like his brother. But the more minutes that passed, the more and more on edge he grew. He hated the idea of Teddy being in pain, and while she was a tough cookie, headaches seemed to hit her really hard.

"Sorry, just the idea of you putting her to bed is kind of funny," Solomon said quickly, holding up his hands in a placating gesture. "Given, ya know, how she is."

Ah, now that he could agree with. Teddy had gotten the flu once, and getting her to slow down for that had been like chasing around a toddler who didn't want to go to bed. "Driven to a fault and willing to put her physical needs aside more often than not?"

"Yup. Exactly."

Silas let out a sigh. He'd really hoped that Frenchie would magically materialize with her bottomless fanny pack of over-the-counter pharmaceuticals. "This is about the only time she'd ever allow me to mother her." And normally Silas was fine with that. He loved how independent his wife was. It also made him feel exceptionally important when she chose to trust him to take care of her. As far as he knew, there was a very short list of people who were given that privilege, and he wasn't about to take it for granted.

But sometimes, usually just when she was sick or injured, he wished she'd let him baby her just a little bit more. As a treat.

"But yeah, Bryant, if you could go ask, that'd be a godsend."

His cousin nodded and stood up from the table. "Walk with me. We'll find out together."

Silas did just that, and he was quite grateful that his cousin didn't dawdle on their stroll. He hurried along, heading straight toward the main house.

Fortunately, they did indeed find Auntie Miller inside, stirring something delicious smelling on the stove with Missy up on a stool, grabbing a giant pitcher from a high cabinet.

"Oh, what can I do ya for, fellows?" Auntie asked, as kind as ever.

"Silas here needs something for a headache."

"A headache? Or is it a migraine?"

Silas had never been so grateful to be surrounded by people who all knew the difference between the two.

"Just a headache so far."

"Okay, I've got some liquid gels, drowsy and nondrowsy. I can also make a tea that's good for headaches as well and won't mix with the medicine."

"That'd be a godsend. I'll get Teddy the meds, walk her to the cabin, then come back for the tea."

"Don't you worry about all that! I'll send one of my boys with a thermos for you. Just get your lovely to bed."

"Thanks, Auntie."

"Of course. Missy, would you go show him the medicine cabinet?"

"Wait, they're in the medicine cabinet?" Bryant interrupted. "Last I checked that was empty."

"Yeah, we emptied those ones out once one of the kids got old enough to reach the bathroom mirror. There's a hidden one in a safe in the basement." Missy got down from the stool and dusted her hands. "Here, follow me."

She set off and Silas did indeed follow her, more than grateful that they had something. He also kept the medicine cabinet thing in mind. While no one in his family other than Simon and Leilani had had a baby yet, it was a good idea to keep in mind.

"You should find whatever you need right here."

"Thanks a million."

"No problem. Tell Teddy I hope she feels better."

Silas gave the woman a nod. While Teddy and Missy weren't exactly best friends, he knew that they got along fairly well whenever they got together. That, and there were always guaranteed to be at least ten or so pictures of them flexing their impressive guns. Before she got pregnant, Ginny would join in too. Although she seemed well on her way through her recovery considering how difficult that process was. Silas wasn't the most informed of the situation, but he did remember Nova baking some macarons for Ginny while she was in the thick of her morning sickness.

Crouching, Silas saw they really did have pretty much one of everything. Rooting around, he picked out two that looked like what Teddy used. Both were liquid gels, but one had something to help her sleep and the other had caffeine. Since she didn't have a full-fledged migraine, he was pretty sure that Teddy would be able to pick out which she preferred.

Closing the safe and making sure to spin the dial once it was shut, Silas hurried back outside. When he arrived at their table, Teddy was pretty much melted against it, her hands over her ears.

Gently, he shook her arm, feeling his stomach turn at the thought of her being in so much pain. He *hated* it. He knew it was silly to be so worked up over his wife having something as simple as a headache, but how could he not?

Actually... now that he thought about it, Teddy had been getting a lot of headaches lately, hadn't she? She'd had one in the car. And a migraine the week before. The more he recalled, the more he realized that for the past month and a half, she'd been having them at least once a week.

And not to mention fatigue too. Teddy wasn't one for naps unless she was on her period, but she'd taken to sleeping in every weekend and napping right after work. He'd just thought that running the business was hitting her hard, considering Andre had retired and her brother's girlfriend was struggling with Crohn's disease, but what if something else was going on?

The thought made nausea rise up within him, but that would have to be something he'd deal with later. For the moment, he needed to get Teddy taken care of and into bed.

"Hey, Teddy, I've got some stuff for you. There's PM liquid gels and extra strength with caffeine. Which do you want?"

"PM," she whispered, one of her hands leaving her head and

laying open on the table. Silas hurriedly placed three of them into her waiting palm, then grabbed the bottle of water that was sitting on the table and handed that to her as well. She lifted her head with what looked like great effort, knocking back the medicine before sinking onto the table yet again.

"Do you want to sit here a few minutes until it starts to kick in?"

"Yeah..."

She was barely audible, but thankfully, Silas had pretty good hearing. He sat down next to her, very gently rubbing her back. He couldn't say quite how long they stayed there, but it was at least fifteen minutes before she drowsily raised her head.

"I... I think I'm ready now."

"Okay. Just take my hand. I'll walk you to the golf cart so we can get you to our cabin. Then you can lie down, okay?"

She nodded, her eyelids fluttering. In the years since they'd been dating, he'd long since learned that Teddy had a little bit of a sensitivity to any sort of sedative. Nothing too scary, but any sort of Melatonin or PM medicine tended to knock her out pretty fast. But hey, at least if she was unconscious, she couldn't be in pain.

Or at least he hoped so.

Careful as could be, Silas slowly led her to one of the four golf carts that were at the edge of the reunion, then drove her to their cabin. They were newer buildings; his cousins having built seven or so of them about four years previous. Definitely a necessity considering how much the family kept growing and that they were all getting along a lot better now. It actually hadn't been that long ago when most of the Millers resented or didn't communicate with the others.

"We're almost there, Teddy."

"Okay."

She leaned against his side, warm and solid, while he finished up the rest of the drive. Parking next to the door, he helped Teddy into the small but cozy cabin and put her to bed. She didn't resist, sleepily muttering something before pressing a kiss to Silas' cheek. It was sweet, and some of the heavy weight inside of him faded.

"Love you," she whispered right before her jaw went slack and her breathing turned to the heavy rhythm of sleep.

"Love you too," Silas answered, leaning down to plant a kiss right on her forehead. Hopefully she would feel better soon.

Before he could even get up and check his phone, a gentle knock sounded at the door. Tiptoeing over, he opened it to reveal Sophia, a broad grin across her face.

"Ma sent me to give this to you."

"Thanks. I'm sure Teddy will appreciate this when she wakes up."

"I know that whenever Ma gives me something when I'm feeling ill, that it always does the job right. She hasn't failed me yet."

"I'm pretty sure the world would invert itself if she did."

"Stranger things have happened, I suppose."

"Well, I'm gonna get back to the party. See you tomorrow?"

"Hopefully, yeah."

Sophia gave the nod then headed off, allowing Silas to close the door. He set the thermos in the kitchen, knowing it would most likely stay warm for hours, then returned to watch the bed.

As soon as they were home, he was definitely going to insist that Teddy get herself to the doctor. Maybe it was morbid, but he couldn't help but think about his uncle to the west, the one who had lost his wife to a disease that came out of nowhere. Silas didn't think Teddy was in that sort of situation, but still... he worried.

For the moment, however, he would just have to content himself with watching over her and making sure she drank the tea as soon as she was awake. At least he was getting to spend his time by her side.

Exactly where he wanted to be.

16

Teddy

"Excuse me, I'm *what!?*"

Teddy stared at the doctor like he'd grown three heads and decided to tap dance in a showgirl outfit. And yet he was standing there like he hadn't just said the most impossible, bizarre sentence that she'd ever heard.

"We've done the test twice to be sure, so it's safe to say that you're definitely pregnant."

Pregnant?

Pregnant!?

Teddy continued to stare at him, her mind spinning, echoing and doing a bunch of complex choreography that made her want to vomit and maybe also fall into the floor.

"But I—"

"I take it this wasn't an expected pregnancy?"

"What?" Her voice sounded hollow in her own ears, like it was coming from several feet from her.

"Was this—"

And then she realized what he actually said, his words hitting her like little bullets, one right after the other. "No. It wasn't."

It felt like she was about three steps behind life, desperately trying to catch up while being completely out of it. The only reason she was at the doctor was for her headaches! She thought it was silly, but Silas had been *real* insistent after they'd come home from his family reunion. Since when did being pregnant give debilitating headaches on the regular? No one had told her that before.

"I understand that this might be a difficult situation—"

"It's not that I'm opposed to children," she interrupted quickly, her mouth moving of its own accord. "But I wasn't ready for them yet. I was thinking a year or so from now, when things are less hectic." Teddy paused for a moment, trying to calm herself down. "I'm on birth control! I've had the implant since I was seventeen and my period cramps were making me miss school."

"Sometimes these things happen, even on birth control. Especially if you're towards the end of your implant's lifespan."

"Oh."

And that was all she could say for a moment. Because reality was slowly sinking in and Teddy found herself looking at an entirely different year than the one she'd imagined.

Things were still so intense! With her father retiring and her taking over the shop, it had already been hectic enough. But then her brother's girl had started getting sick, and that situation was still escalating. The poor sweetheart had only just gotten her diagnosis!

"How am I supposed to run a mechanic shop if I'm pregnant?"

"Pardon?"

"Nothing, I uh... wow. Okay. This is a lot. Is there a way to tell how far along I am?"

"No, we'd need to do an ultrasound for that, which we can schedule for you. In fact, I'd like you to meet up with your OBGYN to start setting everything up."

"Everything? What does that mean?"

"You're going to need to get on a vitamin regimen, set up check-ins and checkups, make a pregnancy plan as well as a birthing one."

And there was that overwhelming feeling again, grabbing Teddy by both of her ankles and yanking her back down into the mire.

"That, uh, kinda seems like a lot."

"It is, and I understand if you're feeling a little anxious, but the faster we get you your information, the more informed you will be about all of your options."

"Right... right. Do I have to do this today?"

"No, of course not. Other than getting the OBGYN visit scheduled, you can set the rest up after you meet with her."

"Okay then. I'd like to do that."

"No problem. In the meantime, I'm going to write you a prescription that should help with your morning sickness and maybe even your headaches. It's the only thing we can do for now until you find out the specifics of your condition."

"My condition," Teddy repeated.

The rest of the appointment was a little fuzzy around the edges, although Teddy did try to type into her phone everything she needed to do.

She'd just found out she was pregnant only minutes earlier and already she had way too long of a list. It seemed impossible, and as she slunk out of the office, she couldn't help but feel like she was in way too deep.

Teddy supposed she didn't have too much to worry about compared to some people. Her husband was filthy rich, after all. But they hadn't talked about having a child together. And as understanding of a fellow that he was, she doubted he wanted baby just yet either.

At least Mrs. Miller was going to be ecstatic. She'd been dropping hints about becoming a grandmother for a couple of years, and while Simon's child had placated her for a while, it was clear she wanted even more grandbabies to spoil.

Somehow Teddy made it home, although she wasn't quite sure how. She was pretty sure she was in shock as she walked up to their wing of the house. When Silas and her had first married, Silas' part of the mansion had been connected to the main area. However, after they'd married and she moved in, she had asked for a bit of privacy. She didn't mind living adjacent to his parents, but she needed at least some space.

And so her husband, her darling husband, had hired an entire team who had separated the wing from the rest of the house on the inside, only a glass greenhouse connecting the two. They had their own entrance, their own smaller drive, and that did just right by Teddy.

But even her lovely home couldn't soothe the daze she was in as she hung up her keys where they belonged and set her cell phone on the credenza.

She was pregnant.

Baby in her belly, eggo is preggo, with child, and up the creek without a paddle. *Her.* Tomboy Teddy. The mechanic with a bad attitude and an even badder bat.

Huh.

And then she just kinda... stood there.

It was like she didn't know what to do with herself. It wasn't like she really had a mother that had ever talked to her about such things. She supposed she could go ask Mrs. Miller but, even though she loved the woman plenty, she really didn't feel close to her in that way.

Suddenly anxious in her own skin, Teddy grabbed her keys and phone right back up before heading out the door.

She went to the shop, the two workers that were there already closing for the night. They'd taken to shuttering early on Mondays, as business was slow and they didn't have enough employees to cover dead time. Teddy hurried in and let them go home early, saying she'd clean up after them. It really was lucky that she'd managed to catch the last appointment in the afternoon. She didn't know what she'd do if it was midday and in the middle of the shop's busiest time.

The solitude helped her think, and for just a little while, she was able to push all the anxiety out of her mind and address the topic more matter-of-factly.

She was pregnant. Alright, it wasn't like she never wanted children. Would it be so bad that it was about a year earlier than she expected? Sure, she had a lot on her plate at the moment, but she had all of the Millers to help. Plus, she was pretty sure she could ask Frenchie and Nova to lend a hand with her brother's girlfriend. Especially since they both had official Texas driver's licenses now.

Yeah, it was going to be survivable. Perhaps even enjoyable. Teddy was just going to have to adapt ahead of schedule. And it wasn't even like it was the hardest sudden change she'd ever gone through. Certainly not.

But...

She really missed her mom.

Later, on one of her rare days off, she was going to need to visit her mother's resting place with some flowers and talk to her. She was going to be so excited; Teddy knew that. But she wished the woman was still around to actually hold her grandchild. For the first time in a long while, she was struck by how unfair her mother's passing was. She'd been so young...

"Teddy? Are you in here? You weren't answering your phone."

Teddy looked up from the toolbox she was organizing to see Silas walking in from the front of the shop, concern written across his face.

Oh. Right.

She had to tell him. She supposed that she could keep it a secret until she found out how far along she was. Hadn't she heard that a third of pregnancies or something had miscarriages in the first trimester? Was she even in the first trimester?

But she realized within a second that she wouldn't be able to do that. She shared pretty much everything with Silas and keeping things a secret from him—even if it was for health reasons—seemed wrong.

"Silas," she murmured, her voice cracking.

She'd never seen his face go gray so fast. One moment he was across the shop, the next he was right in front of her, pulling her into a hug.

"Did the doctor give you bad news? Whatever it is, I'll take care of you, okay? The important thing is we caught it early."

Oh goodness, he was going off the deep end quick. Granted, she couldn't entirely blame him considering he'd already been worried enough to insist that she make herself an appointment. And didn't he have an uncle, the one with all the daughters, who had lost his wife to illness? Cancer maybe?

"Silas, honey. Silas, it's not anything like that." As much as she loved his embrace, she pushed him back just enough so she could look up at his face.

"What is it then? You don't exactly look like it's good news."

"It's not... *not* good news," she said, trying to find the right words. It wasn't exactly something she practiced; telling her husband that she had an unplanned bun in the oven.

"Theodora, you are killing me right now."

Ouch, he was pulling out the full name. She figured she better get it out before she gave the poor man a heart attack.

"I'm pregnant," she blurted finally, bracing herself for the fallout.

There was silence for at least thirty long seconds before he blinked at her, his face blank. "You what?"

"I'm pregnant," she said more firmly, straightening. "I have an appointment to see how far along at the start of next week."

And then slowly, torturously slowly, a grin spread across his features until he was smiling so broadly it was like his face was going to crack. Once more, Silas was pulling her into a hug, spinning her at the same time.

Yikes, he was definitely going to need to stop with that. Nausea set in the moment he set her down, and she had to swallow a mouthful of spit to calm down that automatic response.

"Are you serious?" Silas cried, holding both of her hands with his.

"This isn't really something I'd joke about."

He let out another happy shout, let go of her to run his hands through his hair, then generally didn't seem to know what to do with his arms. Teddy had never expected him to be so excited, but clearly the man was over the moon.

"We're having a baby! I'm gonna be a *father!*"

He leaned in and kissed her all over her face, peppering affection everywhere he could. It lifted a lot of the anxiety from her, and for the first time since she got the news, she actually smiled.

"You are. We're gonna have our own family."

"I can't believe this! At least that explains all the headaches and nausea." More kisses, and then his face grew serious. "Do you need anything? There's medicine for that, right? Do you need me to rub your feet?"

Teddy chuckled gently. "No, I'm sure that'll come later. But the doc gave me a prescription for something to help with the nausea before I meet up with my gyno. Apparently, it's pretty rare for the morning sickness to start up this quickly."

"Don't worry. Whatever you need, I'll take care of it. I'm here for both of you."

"I know you are."

Even *more* kisses and then he was lifting her and spinning her again. "Maybe go easy on that."

"Sorry. Right. Oh! We have to tell my mother! We have to tell my *brothers!*"

"I'm sure they'll be thrilled. But for right now, maybe we could get some dinner."

Silas took his hands in hers yet again, all smiles. "Whatever you want."

"I'm glad you say that, because I've got a particular craving for frozen yogurt with passion fruit boba."

"Sounds like the meal for champions. And maybe afterward, we get something solid into you?"

"I'll do my best," Teddy answered, looping her arm through his. "But my stomach gives no promises."

"That's okay. I know you'll do your best by our child."

Our child.

The words lingered in her head, big and bold with so much meaning behind them. She was going to have a child. And while that might be life-ruining for some people, it wasn't going to be for her. She was going to have a little boy or girl who was well-loved and would grow up with everything she never had.

"Yeah, I *am*." And she meant it. She was going to be the best mother she could be.

She couldn't wait.

17

Sterling

"Forgive my curiosity, but I can't help but ask why you want to go to college now. You've never shown an interest in it before."

Sterling stared at his financial advisor, debating exactly how to answer. But it wasn't like it was some illicit secret, so he decided the truth was best.

"Yes, I want to be more active in my family's business and I need a better base of knowledge. I've shadowed my brothers as best I can, but I'm missing an entire base of information."

"I see. Well, you certainly have plenty of funds to take care of whatever degree you want to pursue. I trust you know that you will not be receiving any sort of financial aid."

Sterling huffed a laugh at that. "I figured as much. Actually, part of what I wanted to talk to you about was setting up a scholarship fund."

"I'm a bit confused. You have all the money you need."

"Oh, I don't mean for me. I want to set up a scholarship fund for other students. Those who might be struggling to make ends meet or otherwise unable to afford their education."

Sterling tried not to take offense to how his advisor's eyes grew wide with surprise. "That's quite a process."

"I figured as much. That's why I'm here. I figure you can take care of all the technical stuff, right?"

"Uh, yes. We'll have to talk peripheral details of what you want, but that is something that I could help set up."

"Good. I wrote up a list of questions, if you don't mind."

Another shocked expression. Sterling knew he wasn't exactly the most active of the businessmen in his family, but it wasn't like he sat around like a bump on a log. Especially not since starting to date Elizabeth. While she didn't demand anything of him, he knew that she wouldn't really get on with someone who had zero ambition.

"You do? Sure, let's start with those."

They ended up spending an hour going over different things and ended up needing to schedule another meeting after the financial advisor was able to set up the preliminary steps, but Sterling left feeling accomplished.

It had been a whirlwind of events since Elizabeth and he had gotten serious. Between his brothers all finding their loves, his cousin getting into a nearly fatal crash, and even little Cici starting to court someone, it seemed like there was always something major going on. Not that Sterling was complaining. But he did realize that everyone in his family was growing, learning, and progressing while he just mostly floated around, helping where he could and supporting Elizabeth.

But it was time to step up and do even more. After all, eventually he wanted to start a family with Elizabeth, but there was stuff he wanted to get out of the way first. Not that he couldn't accomplish anything once they had kids, but there was a certain amount of ease in doing it before any little bundles of joy came bouncing into their lives.

Heading home, he stopped to pick up some treats at a Greek bakery he and Elizabeth both liked. And if he snacked on one of the pieces of baklava in the truck, well... nobody needed to know that. The important part was that he arrived with 90% of the goodies.

Like most of his family, he decided to stay on their property, but unlike the rest of them, he and Elizabeth had elected to build their own home on the opposite end of their quite large tract of land. It wasn't nearly as prestigious as his parents' giant home, but he and Elizabeth didn't need that. They had a plenty large home with five bedrooms. More than Elizabeth had wanted at first, but when he told her it would be for any future children that they might have, she'd begrudgingly agreed. Sterling didn't know if they were going to actually have three children, they'd have to see how they did with one, but he figured those could always become office and craft spaces.

As for his wing of the house, well, Nova had moved into that for a while, but since she and Sal had gotten hitched, the two of them had somewhat combined the space. With limited success. But with Solomon, Sterling, and Simon all in their own homes, the manor was growing increasingly empty. Maybe that was why their mother had become so insistent on grandchildren in the past couple of years. It was like once Simon and Leilani had their little one, she'd gotten a taste of the grandma life and wanted more.

Kicking off his shoes as soon as he was in the door, Sterling headed towards their bedroom. Sure enough, Elizabeth was napping there. She wasn't usually one for mid-afternoon snoozes, but she'd had a pretty long week that included a difficult birth with a horse about three hours away, and a couple of cows with major abscesses and a resistance to antibiotics. And that wasn't even counting the time she spent in digital meetings, many of them with Missy, his cousin-in-law up in Montana who had about a billion and one rescues she was involved in.

"Hey there, sleepyhead. Do you want to keep snoozing or do you want some snacks?"

"Snacks?" she murmured, sitting up. "What'dya get?"

"Some treats from the Greek place we like."

"Really?" She perked up at that, rubbing her eyes as she did. It wasn't often that anybody got to see Elizabeth in any sort of state of disarray, and Sterling felt a certain sort of satisfaction that he got to see it every morning and other bonus times.

"Yup. I've had a good day, so I figure it's worth celebrating the good times, you know?"

"I can get behind that."

"And how are you enjoying your day off?"

"Honestly, I've pretty much just been catching up on sleep."

Sterling nodded, setting his bag on their nightstand. "Did you eat breakfast? I got up before you."

"Um... do I have to answer that?"

Sterling chuckled. "That's answer enough. Come on, scoot over. We'll eat in bed and throw something on the TV like a couple of bums."

"But we'll get crumbs in the bed!"

"Don't worry, I'll wash the sheets."

She chuckled lightly. "Look who's adjusting to life without staff so seamlessly!"

"You say that like I didn't spend the first six months here not even knowing where we put the washer and dryer."

"Well, you've come a long way since then." Elizabeth pushed herself up to kiss his cheek, then did indeed scoot over, allowing him to slide into bed. Maybe it was anticlimactic, but Sterling couldn't think of a better way to finish his day. He was with the woman he loved, enjoying delicious treats while planning his future.

"I met with my financial advisor today."

"And how did that go?"

"Not bad. But he seemed shocked that I wanted to go back to college. Hard not to take it personally."

She reached over and thumbed a piece of flaky filo dough off his chin. "That's because he doesn't know you. But I do, and I'm so proud of you."

Sterling glowed at her praise, looping an arm around her. "Thanks, Elizabeth. That means a lot to me."

"I love you, Sterling. And I'm so impressed with everything you're working towards."

"I love you, Elizabeth," he echoed. "And I'm excited to see just who I'll be too."

They shared a kiss, short and sweet, then returned to their snacks. Elizabeth turned on some fantasy show that she was into, and he settled further into their comfy little nest. And unlike all those years he spent hollow and empty, Sterling finally felt content.

18

Elizabeth

*E*lizabeth drained another bottle of water and sprayed more bug repellent on. "Where did I put that towel?"

"They say you get used to the heat," Sterling mused as he joined her, setting his clipboard down so he could chug some water with her.

"I don't really want to be here long enough to get used to it, but I'm real grateful that our dehumidifier in the hotel works."

The heat in Florida wasn't really any worse than Texas in the summer, but the humidity of it all made it so much worse. It was like she was walking through soup, and it left her way hotter and sweatier than she liked to be. Not to mention the *bugs*. There were so many of them, and of all different varieties. Elizabeth liked animals, liked nature, but even she hadn't been aware there were so many types of annoying, buzzy bugs that liked to get right up in people's faces.

"I hear that," Sterling said before spraying himself as well.

They lingered a few more moments before returning to where Missy was. For being a multimillionaire, the blond sure didn't have any compunction with getting down and dirty. At the moment she was erecting a fence with some of the volunteers from the reserve.

"Hey there! I'll finish this up in a minute, then we'll restart the tour."

"You want some help?" Sterling asked.

"Sure. If you're comfortable."

Elizabeth did her best not to preen, but it wasn't the easiest task. When she had first met Sterling, he never would have volunteered to do such manual work. But he'd grown so much—into a more thoughtful, mature man who didn't even hesitate to help out.

And she liked to think that he'd helped her grow too. Elizabeth felt a little less sharp, like she wasn't necessarily as quick to throw up her walls, and she was much more willing to give someone the benefit of the doubt. Sterling and his family proved to her that there was good in the world, and even extremely flawed people could improve and become truly wonderful human beings.

"Is there something non-technical that I can help with?" Elizabeth asked.

"Nah, you just wait there," Missy answered. "We need your expertise, and the last thing I want is you getting accidentally hurt doing a side job here."

"I mean... could I hold something?" Normally Elizabeth

might have taken a little offense at being pushed aside. But after Missy had told her just how difficult a time the reserve had with trying to recover from the last big storm while also using up all their grant money before they lost it, well, she understood a bit of the paranoia.

"Don't worry. We'll just be another couple of minutes. I thought the two of you would take a bit longer on your break."

"I want to make sure I finish at least half of this walkthrough before the sun starts to set. I've been told the mosquitos get even worse at twilight."

"You're not wrong about that. It's the second time I've been down here, and yet I'm still shocked by the number of bugs that seem to come right out of the ground sometimes."

Elizabeth gave a slight shudder. She wasn't scared of critters, but she wasn't overly fond of parasites or blood suckers.

But true to Missy's word, they did finish the last part up within five minutes, and then they were walking along to the next enclosure.

"Alright, this netted-off area is for the rehabilitation of birds of prey."

"And it's set back here because these are the ones they hope to release back into the wild and they don't want them to get too acclimated to humans, right?" Elizabeth asked, walking along one of the edges. It was quite a large area—which was good—but she needed to see the whole thing.

"Yes indeed. The permanent residents are closer to the center by the headquarters."

Elizabeth nodded, slipping fully into work mode. Her eyes scanned everything, trying to take in every detail she could. The reserve and rescue had done a good job, sure, but it was clear that they were trying to take it to the next level with their expansions, and she was more than happy to help.

As they slowly walked the perimeter, she pointed out different things that could be fixed or enhanced and Sterling dutifully wrote them down. It probably seemed like a little thing to everyone else, but having him around really sped up the whole process. It used to be that Elizabeth would spot something, come to a full stop, write it down, then try to pick back up where she left off. It was easy to get distracted that way, and her hand-writing was bad on a good day, but even more terrible when she was trying to balance her notebook on her knee.

Like usual, Elizabeth sank so deep into her rhythm that she didn't notice how much time had passed until Missy let out a low whistle. "Whoa, would you look at that! The sun's going down."

Elizabeth blinked and glanced towards the sky. She knew Missy wouldn't lie about something like that, and yet she was still shocked when she looked to the sky and did indeed see that darkness was just beginning to set in, its onyx fingers slowly dipping into the coral-stained clouds to bleed into twilight purple.

"Huh. Guess we'll finish this up tomorrow then?"

"Yeah! Again, I really appreciate you volunteering to come down and help with this. You would not believe the hoops they've had to jump through here to try to get any advisor to come down and help."

"You told me about that. Something about someone at the country house giving you trouble?"

"I wish it was that simple. One of the girls here turned down some rich old man who was trying to pick her up, and apparently he was someone with quite a few connections."

Sterling straightened at that, looking up from his notebook with arched eyebrows. "Excuse me, what?"

"Yeah, it's a messed-up situation."

"What's his name? Maybe I should pay him a visit."

Elizabeth didn't approve of violence unless it was absolutely necessary, but she loved that Sterling already had his hackles raised for someone in need.

"If I knew that, I would have long been there. The girl never caught his name, and somehow, he's being more elusive than you'd expect someone like that to be. Usually they're all too happy to gloat about whoever they're exploiting."

The wheels in Elizabeth's head started to turn. "Hmmm, maybe I should do some investigating of my own. I bet I could visit a few exotic vets in the area and see what's going on. I'm not really associated with here like you are, and people won't exactly think of me as your sister on sight."

"What are you talking about? We're basically identical."

That was enough to startle a laugh out of Elizabeth. "You're right. What was I thinking? They'll be able to sus me out on the spot."

There was more joking all around as they headed back towards where they parked their cars, and Elizabeth's feet were grateful once she was off them. But still, her mind was full as she drove to their small hotel.

Apparently, Sterling felt much the same, because almost as soon as they were in the door, he looked to her with a knowing sort of expression.

"You want to stay a couple of extra days and do some investigating?"

"You get me," she remarked, leaning over to kiss him. "And yes. Absolutely."

"We'll figure out who this guy is, and hopefully that'll help Missy and the rest of them." The look of determination on his face was so endearing. Elizabeth didn't think she'd ever been so in love.

"I'm sure we can do it. We make a great team, after all."

When he looked at her, she could see all of his love reflected right back at her. "Yes, we do. Forever and always."

"Forever and always."

19

Salvatore

Sal held his breath, putting all of his concentration into the task at hand. He could feel his heart thundering in his chest, beating its own urgent rhythm that made his entire body tremble. It was somewhat ironic, he supposed, to have all the muscle he did but to still end up shaking like a leaf. His hands, normally so sure and confident, weren't even safe, practically vibrating in his protective gloves.

He could feel sweat beading on his brow, threatening to drip into his eyes, but he couldn't pause long enough to wipe it away. He was almost done with what he needed to do, but if he fumbled at the last moment, it could all turn into nothing.

Worse than nothing, it would be a *mess*. And a waste of time and effort. And while Sal loved taking it easy since he'd stopped trying to compete with Solomon, that didn't mean he liked failing at very important tasks.

Come on, come on. You're almost there!

Finally, he did it, gently setting the soufflé on the kitchen counter. Stepping back, he finally allowed himself to heave a long breath.

"Thank goodness!"

Now that it was safe, Sal allowed himself to feel proud of his work. Although he'd come to love his baking times with Nova and his mother, there were still many things that he considered out of his depth. And soufflés were definitely one of them. But considering it was their first anniversary, he wanted to do something special for her.

They'd already had their big celebration on the weekend, at a fancy restaurant with a carriage ride around the city. They'd done that to accommodate for both of their work schedules, even though it wasn't necessary. They could have just taken off, but Nova was even more insistent about not receiving special treatment like that. It also didn't help that when one of their ranch hands had broken his femur, she'd taken over a lot of his tasks, which required her to pretty much stick to the same schedule that he'd been on.

Nevertheless, the weekend had been wonderful, magical even, and Sal didn't regret one second of it. But he also wanted to do something special for their actual anniversary. So, he'd gotten the idea to bake her a fully English dinner with a *very* fancy dessert.

"My goodness gracious!" Mom whispered, coming into the kitchen. "You've done it! How amazing!"

"The recipe you gave me had very clear instructions," he said with a grin, his pride growing by the second. He didn't want to spill over into cocky, but it was hard not to feel accomplished considering all he'd heard about how hard it was to get the thing right.

Granted, it could still deflate before Nova got done with work, or it could taste horrible. But he was fairly certain it wouldn't.

Or at least he hoped not.

"If you would have told me two years ago that my l'il Sal was going to become a baking wizard, I might not have believed you."

"A baking wizard?" He laughed lightly. "I'm hardly anything like that."

"I don't know. Out of the two of us, you're the only one who's baked a soufflé in the past year."

"Right, but this is for a very special occasion and could have gone very wrong."

"Hush boy, I'm giving you flowers. You can choose to nurture them or not."

Sal rolled his eyes good-naturedly. Ever since Frenchie had taught them about "giving flowers," his mother had been using the phrase nearly nonstop. It was kind of cute, in a parent trying to use young slang kind of way, but also maybe she had a point.

"Fine, thank you for the compliment. I hope Nova loves it just as much as you do."

"I'm sure she will! Would you like me to help set up the smaller dining room for you while you cook?"

"Thanks, Ma. I'd love that."

While Sal set about finishing the Yorkshire pudding with sausage and gravy, his mother gathered all the dishes, glasses, wine, and candles to make it quite the romantic dinner. He was more than a little relieved that she'd decided to help with that particular task, considering he didn't exactly feel overconfident in his table-setting skills. Especially when he was already concentrating so hard on something else.

He remembered when he'd first read about Yorkshire pudding. He'd thought it was some sort of chocolatey dessert. Not so much. Instead, it was a savory sort of not-quite-a-biscuit thing that held the sausage and gravy rather well.

Except the sausage wasn't really anything like breakfast sausage, and instead was similar to a bratwurst. The English sure did have a funny way of going about things, but he hoped he was doing Nova's homeland at least a little justice.

The time rushed by in a blur of sizzling, checking the oven, and plating everything. By the time everything was presentable, it was nearly time for Nova to pop in.

"I better go and make myself scarce. You and Nova have a lovely evening!"

With that she kissed his cheek and hurried out, humming to herself. Sometimes it was hard to tell if his mother was just a hopeless romantic or if she was subtly trying to encourage anything that would result in more grandbabies.

Too bad she wasn't going to really gain much ground that way. Nova had made it clear about no babies until she got her knee more under control and finished her education. Sal couldn't blame her. Considering that her knee would just give out at random times, he could respect why she wouldn't want to waddle around pregnant on that.

And they didn't have any sort of end date for that either. She was still completing her physical therapy, and her doctor had added some acupuncture to her rotation. Sometimes it seemed like she was improving, but because she refused to take things slow, eventually she'd do something or have an accident that set her right back.

But it wasn't the time to worry about that. Instead, Sal focused on getting all the food on the table and covered, then washing his face so he could get changed. While he wasn't going to dress in a tux or anything, he didn't exactly want to have dinner in his grubby baking clothes. Because even with an apron, he wasn't really a pristine cook, and he wanted to look nice for his wife.

He finished just in time, changing his outfit and ending up downstairs in the foyer right as Nova stepped in. She pulled up short at the sight of him, her eyes looking him up and down.

Even after all their time together, Nova still would examine him like she admired him more than any other man. And Sal certainly didn't mind that. He appreciated the raw attraction she had for his body just as much as her blatant approval of his personality. Both were balanced, just how he liked it.

And Sal liked to think she could say the same of him. He loved her body, her thick thighs and just how tall she was. The shape of her face and that intelligent glint that was always in her eye. But he loved *her* too, even without all that. He loved her wit, her kindness, and definitely her perseverance.

"What's going on?" she murmured, looking right exhausted.

"If you'd come with me," he said, giving a bow and guiding her to the smaller dining room towards the back of the main house.

"Is this an anniversary thing? This feels like an anniversary thing."

"It just might be," Sal confirmed, taking his hand as they walked through the house. When they reached their little table all set for dinner, Nova let out an audible gasp.

"Did you do all this?" she asked, eyes wide.

"Mother helped a bit. But I cooked everything."

"Is... Is this Yorkshire pudding and sausages!?"

"And gravy," Sal confirmed, keeping the soufflé in his back pocket. After all, it could have deflated in the time that he'd gone to clean himself up.

"Oh my gosh, Sal, this is amazing. I can't believe you did all this. And on a weekday!"

"I figured it would be nice to have a more lowkey thing, just you and me."

"You're amazing, really."

Nova pulled him into a kiss, her arms around his neck to pull him closer. Sal let himself be moved, loving the contact. That was one of the many things he loved about Nova—her ease with physical touch. He hadn't realized that he'd been touch-starved before, not when his whole life was trying to figure out how to get into his father's good graces and become the number one son. But looking back, he could see how he'd been starved for affection, both emotional and physical. Nova had literally healed him, although sometimes it seemed like she didn't understand how much she'd changed his life.

"Coming from you, I'll take that as quite the compliment."

He pulled her chair out for her, gesturing for her to sit. She did so and shuffled forward as he pushed it back towards the table. Once he was sure she was settled, he went to his own seat and made himself comfortable.

"May I have a plate, kind sir?" Nova asked, batting her eyelashes at him. Sal huffed a chuckle and took the dish from her, filling it up fairly liberally. He might have cooked a lot more than they needed, but oh well, leftovers for the rest of the week.

"This smells *so* good," Nova crooned as he handed the plate back to her. "A lot of English food can be a bit gross or flavorless, but this is a *classic*."

"Good to know," Sal said, filling his own setting. "It was between this or Fish n' Chips."

"You definitely made the better choice. It's surprisingly difficult to get a good fry."

Sal remembered reading that as well, which influenced a lot of his decision. He was glad to know that his resources had been right about so many details. It was hard to tell sometimes on the internet.

The rest of the meal went great, the two of them laughing and talking. By the time their plates were cleared, Sal was feeling quite full and content.

Except there was one more thing to do, wasn't there?

"Well, I think I'm about ready to take a shower and wind down for the night."

"Actually, if you don't mind waiting a moment, I have something to show you."

"What, you have something else stuffed up your sleeves besides those glorious biceps of yours?"

"Believe it or not, I do, Lady Nova."

Nova chuckled and made a gesture for him to get to it. Chuckling, Sal headed to the kitchen. And sure enough, there the soufflé was, looking fully inflated and delicious.

Carefully, he put it onto the serving platter, then took it to the dining room. Nova had turned in her seat so that she was facing him as he entered, and her jaw quite literally dropped.

"Is that what I think it is?"

"That depends. Do you think it's a soufflé?"

"I can't believe you made that! That's such a difficult bake."

"I wanted to do something special. Something to show you how much you mean to me."

"Oh, Sal." Suddenly she was up out of her chair, arms around his neck again and kissing him senseless. "You are wondrous, you know that?"

"Wow, wondrous? We're busting out the big words, aren't we?"

"For you, always."

She kissed him again, and again, and again, until finally his arm holding the serving tray started to get tired. "I should probably set this down."

"Huh? Oh right."

Sheepishly, Nova let go of him, although she did scoot her chair right next to his. Together, the two of them dug into the treat he made. It was simple, but it was so lovely. Sal could envision the rest of their lives full of similar moments. Side by side, just enjoying life together.

It turned out that Happily Ever After wasn't just an event, or a chapter marker in their life. It was an entire state of being, and one that Sal would never take for granted.

He'd lived too much of his life on the dark, negative side of things. But he'd seen the light, and he was going to bask in it with the love of his life.

Not bad, not bad at all.

20

Nova

Consciousness came back to Nova in waves, lapping at her feet, thoughts too far away to make much sense. She felt disconnected from her body in a way that she wasn't used to, like a balloon whose string had been cut, sending her floating up into the upper atmosphere.

Time took a strange tilt to it, syrupy and bendy all at the same time, twisting in on itself until it lost all meaning. But she was aware that she was steadily waking up, bit by bit, until her eyes finally fluttered open. Or at least tried to.

"Oh hey, there you are. How are you feeling?"

Nova recognized the voice, but she couldn't quite get to her brain in order to respond. She also couldn't quite figure out why her eyes felt glued shut or her mouth like the Sahara Desert.

"The doctor said you were allowed some ice chips once you were awake. Would you like some?"

Right! That was Sal and she was in the hospital. She'd gotten surgery on her knee. A new, innovative one that was supposed to really help her. No more dislocations; no more popping in and out whenever it wanted. It had been scary, sure, but Nova had charged into it with her usual self-assuredness.

And now she was waking up after the whole affair. Or at least she hoped it was after. If it wasn't, well the surgeon certainly would have a lot of explaining to do.

"You there, Nova?"

She nodded, or at least she was pretty sure she nodded, because the shadow over her moved away and an uncertain amount of time later, something cold was being placed against her lips.

Thankfully Nova was able to open her mouth enough to accept the bit of what she guessed was an ice chip, and *goodness,* she didn't anticipate just how good it felt to have the cool wetness creep across her sandpaper-coated tongue.

"There you are. Just suck on that for a bit and you can answer once you're ready. Just make sure you don't fall asleep with it in your mouth, okay?"

Another maybe nod as Nova worked on the tiny piece of ice. It melted far too soon, and she opened her mouth for more. Naturally, Sal was right there, putting another one on her tongue.

The hydration definitely seemed to do her well, and she felt more like a human by the second. After her fourth bit, she managed to clear her throat and move her mouth in something akin to speech.

"...Sal?"

"Hey, Nova! How are you? You feeling okay?"

"I'm... alive," she murmured. "Did... uh, how's my knee?"

"Doctor said you did great in the surgery. But is there a reason you're keeping your eyes closed? Do you want to go back to sleep?"

"Stuck," Nova muttered before realizing that wasn't quite a real answer. "They're stuck."

"Stuck? Oh! Hold on, let me get a warm washcloth for you."

He left her side again but was back only moments later, pressing something deliciously warm and soothing across her eyes. At first nothing happened, but as the seconds passed, the glue-like substance sealing her lashes together faded, allowing her to slowly blink.

"I see you looking around under there. You ready for me to take the cloth off?"

Nova nodded and Sal slid the fabric off her face. But almost immediately she was blinded by just how bright the room was and her lids slammed shut again.

"Oh, sorry! Let me turn the lights off, then we'll try again."

A lot of feelings were setting in on Nova all at once, and it struck her as so sweet how her husband was rushing to take care of her. She'd read all sorts of horror stories on the internet about inattentive partners and the like, but Sal wasn't anything like that. No, he was giving her precious liquid, warm washcloths, and even managing the light levels of her austere hospital room.

"How's that?" he asked, coming back to the side of her bed.

Nova still couldn't quite handle the whole human speech thing though, so she settled for a thumbs up. But even that simple gesture had him beaming from ear to ear.

Goodness, he was so wonderful. Suddenly Nova had the urge

to eat him up with a spoon. But then she wouldn't have him anymore, so maybe less eating and more hugging. Once she had control of her body again, that is.

"So, the doctor should be back within a few hours to catch you up with everything that's happened and all of your aftercare. You'll probably be here overnight, but after that, I'm taking you home where I'm going to spoil you rotten and there'll be nothing you can do about it."

Nova managed a sound that was some approximation of a weak chuckle. It was almost like the plot of *Misery*, but totally inversed. Or maybe it wasn't, and the doctors just needed to reduce her pain medicine dose a little. Although more of her mind was returning to her, she still felt a little... groggy, to put it lightly. Her vocabulary apparently wasn't totally loaded in yet.

"Would you like a couple more ice chips? You can't have too many, but I'm sure a little bit extra won't hurt."

Nova nodded again, her mouth still feeling a little sandy, and Sal happily fed her one chip after another, not seeming to care that it took her a couple of minutes for each tiny bit. When her mouth was too cold to enjoy the hydration, she shook her head and Sal backed away.

"You can go back to sleep if you want. It's important you get your rest. Don't you mind me; I'll be right here when you wake up. Mom too, if I'm being honest."

Nova nodded, her eyelids already starting to flutter. But just as she felt like she might be slipping off into oblivion, an old flash of guilt filled her. She remembered when she'd been younger and had her first unsuccessful knee surgery. Her family had been too busy to visit in the hospital when they kept her overnight, and they'd been irritated that she needed so much help afterward. They rushed her into doing everything for herself, telling her that she was being greedy, that she was *inconvenient*. So, she'd tried to do everything herself in an effort not to annoy them.

"Sorry I'm being so needy," she murmured, her stomach flipping in a way that her pain medicine did *not* like.

"What?" Sal was back over at her side in just seconds, and even as woozy as she was, Nova could make out the concern as clear as day on his face.

"M'sorry," Nova muttered, more shame swamping her. Maybe if she could learn to slow down or treat her body right, she wouldn't be in such a position. Wouldn't always be inconveniencing every single human around her.

Ugh.

Ugh.

But Sal took her hand in his, so much compassion and admiration in his eyes. Surely that couldn't be all for her.

"Nova, you have nothing to be sorry for. I love you, and that means I'm going to take care of you. And for what it's worth, I think it's incredibly brave of you to have this surgery."

Nova's heart fluttered in her chest, but at the same time, part of her mind told her that couldn't be true. That no one would think that she was worth all that effort.

"Besides, if you think that I'm not looking forward to having you all to myself and pampering you as much as I can, you're crazy. By the time you're all healed up, you're going to be spoiled rotten."

"You mean it?" Nova whispered, knowing that she sounded a bit childish but not caring. She had goodness knew how many pain meds pumping through her system and a few screws in her knees.

"Of course." He leaned down and pressed the gentlest of

kisses to her cheek. "I love you, Nova. And this is just one more step in our story together."

"I love you too."

Exhaustion flooded her, along with the warm comfort of knowing that she was cared for. Eyelids fluttering, Nova let herself drift off, knowing that she was in good hands.

21

Simon

"Honey, where's the bug repellent?"

Simon set down the cooler he was lugging from the car, catching his breath for a moment. When did he get so out of shape?

"It should be in your backpack. Green can."

"Thanks!"

His wife emerged from their tent with their toddler on her hip, lavender backpack in her other hand.

"I know it's stinky, but trust me, you're gonna want this," she cooed to their little guy. He was a chunky thing, with Leilani's dimples and Simon's eyes. It was hard not to get completely distracted by his adorableness, but Simon was forcing himself to finish unloading the car before he asked to hold his son.

"I'll be right there, Hilo, I promise."

"Stop trying to be his favorite," Leilani said, sticking her tongue out.

"Oh my love, I don't have to *try.*"

Somehow his wife got a hand free to throw a small stick at him, which he dodged with little trouble, a laugh bubbling up out of his mouth. It felt good to just kick back and have a weekend to themselves. While he loved visiting the islands to see her family, they'd been involved in a lot of things. From helping the community organize their protests to him learning about her culture. Things were certainly a lot different on the islands than on the mainland, and sometimes it overwhelmed him. Sure, Simon had taken time off from college to travel the world, but it was one thing to move through a different culture and an entirely different thing to marry into it.

"Show off," Leilani grumbled good-naturedly, handing their baby over to him. Never in a million years had Simon expected to be the first in his chunk of the family to have a kid, but it had happened almost immediately after their marriage. But he didn't mind. He'd taken his time to wander the world and be on his own much more than his brothers had. While it had certainly been enlightening, and he didn't regret it at all, he was much more ready to settle down into the rest of his life than his siblings were.

"You know it," he shot back, taking their son. "Hey there, little guy. Are you excited for your first time camping?"

Despite all their time bouncing between the beauty of the islands and the pleasantness of home, their little family cluster hadn't actually taken any time to grab a tent and go off into the wilderness. Well, demi wilderness. They were only about twenty minutes off the beaten path and still in a somewhat popular camping location, but still, it was nice to get back to the simple things in life.

Not to mention that it was a lovely callback to when they'd set up a trap for Leilani's ex. That scumbag had been a real piece of work, and although maybe pretending to be dating the beautiful woman hadn't been the most elegant way of going about things, Simon was quite happy with how things had turned out.

Hilo let out a gurgling coo, making Simon's heart surge in his chest. He didn't know if it was scientifically possible that he had the most adorable baby in the world, but he was pretty sure that he had the most adorable baby in the world.

Objectively, of course.

"Alright, will you hold his nose?" Leilani asked, the can in her hand.

"Roger-Wilco."

Simon gently pinched his son's nostrils, crossing his eyes to distract him from the strange sensation. Leilani quickly rushed around them in a tight circle, spraying a right cloud of the sensitive-skin, baby-safe bug spray. Normally Simon didn't like using such things around their baby, but considering the insane pest count the past two summers, he preferred to play it safe and make sure he didn't get too bitten.

He supposed that they could have just not camped at all, but he and Leilani really needed the break away from everyone and all the demands of their life. Sure, they had it relatively easy compared to many people in the world. They never had to worry about money, and they could take off to the islands almost any time they wanted. But between their obligations to their families, as well as all the community things they were trying to build with his brothers, it certainly was a lot all on one plate.

"Alright, I'll take him back if you want to finish emptying out the van and setting up the fire pit?"

"Sure, sounds like a plan."

Although Simon was remiss to let his son go, if they wanted to have a good trip, he needed to unpack all the things they'd brought.

Whistling to himself, he got the last of the coolers, their mosquito net, and then the stakes for the fire pit. He was pretty impressed that Leilani was able to set up their tent all by herself with Hilo on her hip, but apparently the little man had enough of cooperating by that point because he was fussing the entire time Simon was setting up their fire pit.

"Come on, baby boy, what's the matter? You were being so good earlier!"

"He's probably hungry," Simon said. "He napped through his last snack time, right?"

"Yes, the car always puts him to sleep. Is the apple sauce in the red cooler?"

"No, the blue one. Blue for cool."

"Right, right, I knew that. Sometimes I feel like I still have pregnancy brain."

Simon nodded, returning to finish building their fire pit. Leilani did have a pretty hard time during her pregnancy with brain fog. From putting her phone in the freezer and accidentally leaving their car running in the driveway, she spent a lot of time confused and upset with herself. Simon had tried to be as supportive as he could, but he knew his wife had quite the independent streak and she hated feeling like a burden.

Even after Hilo was born, he hadn't exactly been a sleeping champion. Although Simon and Leilani took equal turns, the constantly interrupted sleep had extended her brain fog for even longer. Thankfully that era seemed to be mostly over, with Hilo having figured out that sleep was pretty cool.

"Eh, it's an easy thing to forget," he soothed. Because it was. If Simon hadn't been using the system since he was a teen, he may have forgotten too.

Thankfully, the applesauce seemed to do the trick, and Hilo began to settle yet again. Once he was no longer fussing, Leilani set out their thick blanket and let him have his play and waddle time. Hilo wasn't exactly the most intrepid of crawlers or walkers, but he did well enough that his doctor wasn't worried about it so neither was Simon.

Besides, one of his favorite activities was sitting on the ground and having his son waddle over to him, clumsy feet not quite sure as he tottered this way and that. It wouldn't be long before he was old enough to talk, then run, then go to school, and Simon had no idea what to think of that.

Finally, the fire pit was fully built and lined with the proper rocks, and he could sit down to enjoy himself. Plopping himself right on the blanket, he opened his arms.

"Come to Daddy!"

Hilo let out a gurgling sort of coo and did just that, crawling towards him.

"No fair!" Leilani complained between her chuckles. "He never just comes to me like that. I think I need to remind him that I carried him for nearly ten months."

"I'm sure he'll get some perspective when he's older," Simon said, picking up his son when he was within arm's reach and holding him to the sky. "Until then, I'm gonna milk this for all it's worth."

"Fair enough. But with our next one, *I'm* going to be the favorite!"

"Next one?" Simon said, a slow smile curling across his features as their son began to laugh. He always loved being lifted into the air, then pulled back down. "Are we there yet?"

Simon wasn't going to lie; he'd taken to being a father better than he had ever expected. Something about having a little one around made him want to be better, more patient, and more ambitious. He owed Leilani for all of that, and he wasn't going to forget it.

"Actually, I have a present for you."

Abruptly, Leilani was on her feet, going over to her personal bag while Simon watched curiously. Something was definitely up. It wasn't anywhere near his birthday or their anniversary, so what could she be getting?

She returned a few moments later with a small but long box. If Simon didn't know better, he would think it was a necklace. But he wasn't much for jewelry and his wife knew that, so he doubted she'd gotten him anything like a locket or gold chain. Maybe a pooka shell necklace? He'd seen plenty of those when he was on the islands, but they weren't quite his style.

"Here you are," she said, handing the neatly wrapped thing over. Simon took it, trading Hilo for the gift. He clapped his chubby little hands like he was in on the whole thing, which only made Simon that much more curious.

Pulling at the ribbon, he undid the bow, then cautiously opened the box. Naturally there was a layer of tissue paper on top, and he set that aside to reveal—

"Is this a pregnancy test?"

Leilani nodded—hope, worry, and anticipation all written across her beautiful features. Simon's heart quickly began to thunder, and he picked up the test with slightly shaking hands.

Sure enough, there was a plus sign sitting right there, clear and legible.

"Are we going to have another baby?" he asked, knowing his voice trembled but not caring in the slightest.

And Leilani, gorgeous, wonderful Leilani, nodded her head vigorously. "We are! Baby number two is about seven months away."

Simon surged forward, pulling her and their little one into a hug. He couldn't believe it; he was going to be a dad *again!*

"Are you excited?" she asked, eyes wet with tears.

"More than you could ever know."

22

Leilani

𝓛 eilani groaned, her stomach churning as she caught a random scent. What that scent was, she couldn't say, but it wasn't great.

And by wasn't great, she meant that it was headache-inducing, stomach-twisting, leg-shaking awful. Covering her mouth, Leilani rushed to the kitchen, grabbing the mints that Simon had set there the previous week. It was one of the few things they found that could curb her nausea when it got going.

Thankfully, Leilani didn't have anything technically wrong with her. No Hyperemesis Gravidarum, no gestational diabetes, no blood clots, or anything like that. But having nothing wrong with her didn't mean anything was *easy*. While little Hilo had been fairly straightforward, whoever was baking in Leilani's oven was putting up a fight. She had some fairly intense morning sickness that came and went whenever it pleased, and some extreme smell sensitivities. Her feet were swelling up way earlier than they had the first time, and her weight was... being weird. She'd gain the right number of pounds for where she was at only to suddenly shoot past it, but before she could stress about that, she'd plummet back down again. The yo-yoing didn't seem very healthy to her, but her doctor was staying on top of it. He did have her on easy tasks and getting plenty of bed rest, as well as a pretty strict regimen of vitamins, but until something conclusive happened, that was it.

Which was nerve-wracking, to say the least. Leilani *loved* being a mother. Hilo had broadened her world in ways that she didn't think were possible. So when she found out she was pregnant again, she'd been elated. She still was excited, but she was worried that things were going to get worse, and she wouldn't be able to be a proper parent to either her son or her new child.

"Ready for your appointment?" Simon asked, coming down the stairs with Hilo in his arms.

"Huh? Oh yeah." Leilani grabbed a few extra mints and shoved them into her pocket. "It's ultrasound day, isn't it?" She didn't know why she asked, she knew that it was, but it just seemed like something to say. Her nerves were shot at whatever it was she smelled and her body's visceral reaction.

"Yup! We get to find out if we're having a little girl or a little boy!"

If there was one thing that could pull Leilani out of her growing spiral, it was seeing Simon be so excited about their coming child. His joy was infectious in the best way possible, and it settled the trembling nerves within her.

"What do you think of that?" Leilani asked Hilo. "You want to have a little brother or sister?"

Hilo let out a happy shriek. Leilani's ears didn't really enjoy that particular sound, but her heart sure did. Could their boy get any cuter? It didn't seem likely. But maybe she was seeing things with rose-colored glasses.

"You think he'll be a little jealous?" Simon mused, grabbing the rest of Hilo's things they needed to head out.

"Nah, I'm sure he'll like having a little minion around to influence."

"You make him sound like some sort of evil villain."

Leilani laughed. "No, he's definitely a charming sort of anti-hero."

Leilani narrowed her eyes at her husband. "Have you been playing those online role-playing games with your cousin again?"

"...maybe. Hilo likes all the pretty colors."

"Uh-huh, I'm sure that's what it is."

But it was a good-natured ribbing between the two of them, and they continued to banter all the way to their SUV. Leilani got into the passenger seat while her husband put their child into his car seat. Normally that was her job, but the further she got into her pregnancy, the more Simon began to wordlessly help her with taking care of the little things.

She was blessed, so incredibly blessed. She tried not to think of her ex that much, but sometimes she couldn't help but compare Simon to him. Because with every day that passed, it was obvious that the Miller son truly loved her, through and through. He helped her without complaining. In fact, he seemed happy to aid her. And he looked at her every day like she was a wonderful presence that he enjoyed being around.

When she put up a barrier, when she said she didn't want to do something, he respected that. There was no coercion, no threats. He didn't insult her body and tell her she needed to lose weight. In fact, he made it plenty clear just how much he was attracted to her, even with her stretch marks from her first pregnancy, her hormonal acne, and her sore feet.

She loved him. She loved him so much that sometimes it hurt, but it was a pain that she never wanted to get rid of.

"Alright," he said, hopping into the driver's seat and cutting off her sappy thoughts. Probably better that she not linger on them much longer anyway. Another side effect of her pregnancy was the ability to burst into tears at a moment's notice. Just a couple of days ago, a butterfly had landed on their window garden while she was loading up the dishwasher and that had *really* gotten the waterworks going. And a few days before that, she'd cried because she'd thought about Hilo being bullied when he went to school for looking mixed.

Sure, a possibility, but probably not one to weep over considering he was just barely past two.

"You ready to go?"

Leilani nodded and they drove off. As usual, the car ride put Hilo to sleep almost instantly, which let her doze a bit in the passenger's seat. While she wasn't nearly as sleep-deprived as she had been since the last trimester of her previous pregnancy or Hilo's first six months of life, Leilani still loved a good nap whenever she could get one. And with their new baby growing inside of her, she knew that her fatigue was only going to increase.

Simon shook her gently when they arrived at the hospital, and she groggily got out of the car while he collected Hilo and their bags. Not for the first time, she was immensely grateful for her husband. Who would have thought that the young, dashing patron who came into her diner would end up changing her life and taking care of her so tenderly?

Sometimes that life seemed miles away, tucked somewhere

between a fever dream and a Saturday morning cartoon. Other times it seemed far too close, and like one false move would send her tumbling back into the awful.

Thankfully, that fear of backsliding had largely faded with the birth of Hilo, usually only raising its ugly head after a nightmare or a particularly vicious flash of anxiety. And Leilani hoped it kept fading until the worse parts of her past were barely more than shadows, eclipsed by the wonder of her present.

And what a present it was. She couldn't help but marvel as she went into the hospital hand in hand with her husband, Hilo chattering happily from his harness on Simon's chest. While the boy could walk much more steadily than even a few months earlier, he didn't do well with long jaunts, and even with how close they parked in the hospital's garage, there was still a bit of a trek to the office they needed to get to.

It was a miracle that no scents or sounds set Leilani off on their walk, and she was more than grateful to sink onto her rear into the first chair she found in the obstetrician's office.

"Don't you need to check in?" Simon asked, setting Hilo down in her lap and their diaper bag at his own feet.

"Will you go up there for me? I can wave from here."

"Gee, you that tired, hun?"

Leilani nodded. "Just can't seem to get my energy up lately."

"This seems a little more intense than your last pregnancy."

Leilani felt relieved at him confirming exactly what she had been thinking. She wasn't sure why, but it was so easy to doubt herself when it came to her pain and energy levels. "Yeah, it seems like it."

"Huh. You think we should mention that to the doctor?"

"I'll try to make sure to do that, but feel free to step in if I forget."

"Of course. Whatever you need."

And she believed it.

Simon went about checking her in and Leilani made sure to wave to the receptionist with a smile. She knew she'd have to head over eventually, but the extra minutes off her feet were the perfect respite. And if she also dozed off for a minute or two, well, she was in the perfect place for nobody to judge her.

After a bit of signing in and busywork, Leilani ended up in a room, waiting for the ultrasound tech. Simon was playing with Hilo, keeping her son occupied while she changed into the uncomfortable gown and sat on the table.

She was nervous, and not quite sure why. All that was happening was an ultrasound, nothing invasive, no blood draws, no uncomfortable tests. She should have been excited. She was going to find out if they were having a boy or girl.

Well, she supposed that she had been reading too many books and articles about genetics. No one had ever told her that having more knowledge would end up giving her more anxiety. She'd been much less stressed during her first pregnancy, when she'd been so busy reading about the basics that she hadn't had time to research much more complicated fare.

"Hello there, Mrs. Miller! How are we feeling today?"

Finally, the ultrasound tech came in, looking pleasant and refreshed. Leilani remembered back when she didn't always have bags under her eyes or a weariness to her joints.

"Pretty exhausted, I'm not gonna lie."

"Oh? Did we stay up too late watching a movie?"

"I wish. I actually slept for almost nine hours. But I'm still so run down."

"Huh, fatigue is definitely a common part of pregnancy, but

make sure you tell the doctor when she comes in. For the moment, how about I get you all set up to see your baby?"

Oh, right. That was the whole reason that she was there. Nodding, she laid back and let the woman buzz around her, getting everything set.

There was a pleasant sort of familiarity to it, and Leilani let herself drift, listening to the tech, Simon, and Hilo. None of them were being loud, exactly, but the little noises that came from them were comforting in a way. A baby's laugh, her husband saying nonsense things, the woman's finger dragging down a checklist to make sure she wasn't missing any steps. It grounded Leilani, pulling her out of the cloud of anxiety and back into her body.

She was in a happy moment, and she should enjoy it instead of worrying about everything that *could* be.

"Alright, time for the gel. It'll be a little bit cold at first but shouldn't feel that way for long."

Leilani lifted her gown so that her slightly bulging belly was exposed. She knew it was going to get a lot bigger, as long as her weight could regulate, that is.

"So, do you have all of your questions ready for the doctor?" the tech asked.

"Yeah, my husband has a list."

"Oh, fantastic! It's good to come prepared."

"I try my best."

The woman nodded and put the cold gel on Leilani's belly, spreading it around with the wand. Leilani watched the screen dutifully, even though she wasn't really well versed enough to quite understand what was showing on the screen without the tech's help.

She was aware of Simon scooting closer, however, and she

reached out to hold his hand. He took it in hers, his palm so warm and broad, and the physical touch helped her settle further.

"Okay, there we go. I've found your little one. Let's see what kind of details we scope out."

The woman's voice was pleasant, but not falsely so, and Leilani studied the screen as the tech pointed with her free hand. "Oh, look! I see a little foot!"

Leilani had to fight not to lean forward and press her face to the screen. "Feet already?"

"Yup! Right there, if you can see that. Looks like your baby has a primo spot right on top of your bladder."

"Don't I know it," Leilani said with a huff. While the child had yet to start kickboxing her insides like their brother had, she had begun to feel a slight bit of pressure right around that area.

"Okay, moving on, there's a little arm, right there. And oh! Look! Its head. And there's its other arm."

Leilani felt the tears coming on again, no surprise, but how could she not be emotional when there was her baby, all pixelated in gray and white in front of her? She couldn't believe it. All the nausea, the fluctuating weight and the worry were worth it, just to see her healthy baby.

"Now, let's see if they're willing to let us get a peek at their sex. Last ultrasound we talked about how they sometimes can be a bit shy, right?"

Leilani nodded. "Hilo liked to cross his legs almost every time we were in here."

"Is that so?" The tech looked to Leilani's son, who was tugging at Simon's hair, clearly perplexed as to why he wasn't the center of attention.

"Oh yeah," Simon said with a chuckle. "That's part of how he got his name. Since we didn't know what was going to happen, we decided on a traditional Hawaiian name if he was a boy, and an old family name if she was a girl."

"Ah! Looks like your baby isn't feeling as contrary as their brother. I'll have the doctor double-check this and tell you the sex. You did want to know that, yes?"

"Very much so," Simon answered eagerly, bouncing Hilo on his knee.

"Perfect. Just gotta do a little more looking. You've got a lovely sized baby here. And look! There's another arm."

"What?" Leilani said sharply, her head perking up at that.

"Look," she pointed to an entirely different area. "Right there, a well-formed arm."

"...that's the third arm," Simon remarked slowly, seeming to catch onto exactly what Leilani was jolted by.

"Pardon?"

"That arm. It's the third one you've pointed out."

"Was it?" The tech looked perplexed then continued to search around a minute. Suddenly the fact that she couldn't tell any direct information to them grated at Leilani's nerves. Was something wrong with her baby? Did they have an extra limb? Honestly, she could live with that. There were amputations, or plenty of options if it was a healthy bonus arm. But what if it was a sign of something worse? What if it made her baby non-viable?

"Ah, alright. You just sit tight and I'm gonna go grab the doctor."

"Wait, you have to get the doctor right now!?" Alarm bells began to go off in earnest inside her head, her heart thundering in her chest.

"Don't worry, we'll be right back. You just sit tight with your family."

With that the woman hurried out and Leilani was pretty certain she was going to throw up.

"Simon," she whispered, feeling like her world was collapsing in on her. She really needed to stop reading so many medical journals. What if her baby's brain had stopped forming? What if it had some sort of chromosome formation that would end their life before it began? What if she had done something wrong to cause the issue? Would she ever be able to forgive herself!?

"Hey, hey, it's alright. I'm right here." Simon was up on his feet and standing right beside her in a second, Hilo balanced perfectly on his hip. "I'm sure it's nothing."

"A tech doesn't leave the room for *nothing*."

"She does if she's made a mistake and mentioned an extra arm when the baby just happened to move. I'd be pretty embarrassed too."

"I don't think that's it."

Nevertheless, Simon continued to comfort her right up until there was a sharp knock on the door.

"Come in."

Leilani felt like she was going to burst when the doctor stepped in. The woman was all smiles, so surely that had to be good. Right? *Right?*

"It's good to see you, Mrs. and Mr. Miller. So, there's a couple of things I want to address about your pregnancy needs and symptoms, but I want to start off by saying your babies are in fine health."

Wait... what?

"Babies?" Leilani asked, feeling like her voice was outside of her own body.

"Yes, both of them! Congratulations, you two, you're having twins!"

PART III

BRIDES OF MILLER RANCH, N.M. WRAP-UP

23

Charity

Charity's leg bounced up and down as she waited for the social worker to pull up to the house that she and Alejandro had built together. She hadn't been so nervous in years, and she didn't mean to end up sitting in her dining room, just staring at her phone, but that was exactly where she had ended up.

"How long can it take to drive here from the city?" she muttered to herself, checking her phone again, but there wasn't any sort of updated ETA.

So her leg continued to bounce and her teeth worried at her nails. She'd largely stopped with that terrible habit, but every now and again, it would rear its head. And considering that she'd been waiting a year and a half for this day to arrive, she was very anxious indeed.

But finally, finally, she heard the crunch of wheels on their drive and her phone buzzed with the text that she'd been anticipating for over two hours.

WE'RE HERE.

JUMPING TO HER FEET, Charity rushed to the front door of their house, pausing right before opening it. Looking to her mirror, she gave herself a final look over to make sure she was presentable.

"Take a breath, Charity. He's gonna be more scared than you are." Nodding to herself, Charity opened the door.

And there he was, standing right next to his social worker, looking up at her in shock. It wasn't the first time they'd met, not at all. It was actually their third time, the first being in a restaurant, the second being at his foster home.

"Hi there, Jadyn. It's good to see you again."

"Is this really your home?" he blurted, cutting off whatever the social worker had been about to say.

"It's our home, if you'd like to stay here."

The boy looked past her, curiosity and wonder across his features. He was a small kid, for being ten. He had dark skin with a rich, red tone to his warm, brown tones, while his hair was shaved close to his head. While Charity didn't know everything from his file, she did know that he had issues with pulling his own follicles out due to the severe neglect he'd gone through. His lashes had returned since she last saw him, but his eyebrows were still sparse and patchy. Charity hadn't even known that was a thing that could happen, but apparently the prolonged exposure to lice, fleas, and his general anxiety had caused the habit.

"I..."

"How about we go in and Mrs. Lumis-Miller here will give you a tour? Then we'll talk and make sure you're comfortable before I leave."

The boy nodded, his expression shifting to suspicion and trouble. Charity's heart couldn't help but ache for him. Clearly, he'd been through so much.

"My husband, Mr. Alejandro, is finishing up some schoolwork with our daughter upstairs. We figured you'd want some time to yourself to settle in before having to socialize."

The boy nodded, following his social worker as Charity stepped back to let the woman in. Charity hated that the boy was clearly on edge, but it was a necessary evil. Hopefully, in time she would be able to prove to him that he had nothing to be afraid of. He was going to be a beloved part of their family, supported and cared for.

"You sure this ain't a hotel?"

"No, it's our home," Charity tried to say with all the warmth that she could muster. "We actually built it ourselves."

"You did?" Jadyn asked, eyes wide. "You a carpenter?"

"No, more of a general handyman. But I didn't do it on my own. We hired lots of people to help."

"What about your husband, the model guy?"

Charity couldn't help but blurt out a laugh at that. "Alejandro isn't a model. He's a doctor actually."

"A doctor..." the kid murmured, looking around even more resolutely. "So y'all are rich, rich."

Charity didn't think that it was necessary to tell him that

while Alejandro was well off, *she* was the one who was quite wealthy, and just nodded. "We do very well for ourselves."

"Huh."

"If you'd like to set your suitcase to the side, I'm sure Mrs. Lumis-Miller here would love to show you around."

"We'll just avoid Alejandro's home office for now. That's where he and Savannah are."

"And that's your real kid?"

Oh, Charity may have been incredibly new at being an adopted parent, but even she could hear that insecurity.

"If you mean if she's my biological child, no. She's Alejandro's. I married into their family."

"What happened to her real mama?"

"I *am* her real mama. But her biological mother passed when she was very young."

"Oh. That's sad."

"It is, but it all allowed us to find each other."

The kid nodded his head sternly, and Charity knew he was indeed taking her seriously. She hoped that her words brought him comfort, because goodness knew he probably needed it considering his journey. He'd been out of his situation for nearly two years, but considering he'd been in three different foster homes, she doubted he'd had the therapy and time to recover from a lot of what he'd experienced.

Slowly, Charity began to show him around, walking through the dining room, the living room, the kitchen and the bathroom on the lower floor. She also showed him the basement steps but didn't go down, figuring that could be something for another day.

"You ready to go upstairs?"

Another nod, and the three of them journeyed to the second floor. There she showed him the door to the master bedroom, opening it so he could glance inside but not really leading him inside. Then there was the upstairs bathroom, Savannah's room, Charity's office, the playroom, then the two guest bedrooms. Then they reached the very last door, and Charity pushed it open with a flourish.

"And this is your room!"

Jadyn walked inside cautiously, like he expected it to secretly be a portal to something truly terrible, and he froze a single step in the door.

"Do you need me to turn on the lights?" There was sunlight streaming in through both of the windows, but maybe that wasn't bright enough. So Charity quickly flicked the switch, allowing the room to be fully illuminated.

"This is really for me?" Jadyn asked, his voice quiet.

Charity's heart probably could have broken right then and there. Under the advisement of the social worker, they hadn't gone all out. He had a nice bed, sure. A dresser. A bookshelf, some toys. No electronics—those were in the playroom. A mirror. Sure, the closet had clothes and so did the dresser, but he didn't know that.

"Of course. I realize that it's not super personal, but I figured that we could go shopping for any posters or action figures you like. Or even different blankets if you want?"

"Uh, okay."

The boy definitely seemed to need to think for a bit, so Charity looked to the social worker. "You said there were some things we needed to discuss?"

"Yes, some finer details, doctor information, everything you need as a parent."

Charity nodded. "Hey, Jadyn, would you like to have some alone time in here to unpack while we go talk?"

"Yeah. That, uh, that'd be good."

"Alright. And you don't have to stay in your room, just so you know. If you want to leave, you can come down at any time. And if you don't want to leave, that's fine too. Just please don't go into other people's rooms without them there."

"Okay."

Charity started to go, before pausing again. "You also have open access to the playroom. You don't have to ask unless it's during the school week when you have homework."

"I'm gonna go to school?"

"Yes, once you're ready. But there's no rush, okay? We'll just take things a day at a time."

"You're doing great," the social worker whispered, making Charity flush.

"Okay."

"Alright, I'll see you again soon."

Charity and the social worker went downstairs without much fuss. Part of her was worried about leaving Jadyn alone in their house, but she could tell he needed some space. She couldn't imagine the life he'd lived that had led him into her family, but she could be patient.

So she and the social worker talked about more practical details, the woman handing over Jadyn's full medical files and informing her of the finer details of his needs. They ended up taking a good hour or so before the woman said that she felt comfortable leaving for the night, but she would be back in three days just to check on things, then two weeks after that. Charity didn't know if it was common for a caseworker to be that involved, but she got the impression that it wasn't.

Not that Charity minded. As far as she was concerned, Jadyn deserved all the extra effort and care.

"Jadyn, would you come down please?" the woman called to the upstairs. There was a minute or so of nothing, and for a moment Charity was worried that something had happened, but then the young man was slowly descending the stairs. "I'm going to head out, so I'd like to say goodbye."

"Okay."

He wasn't the biggest talker, but Charity already knew that. Back when they first met in that restaurant, he'd said maybe three words. She took it as a win that he'd already said multiple sentences to her in such a short amount of time.

"I'll be back in a few days, so don't you worry. Do your best to settle in here, but you have my phone number if you need it."

"I know."

"Okay then. I'll see you later, young man."

They didn't hug, but they did share a stiff handshake before the woman headed out. Charity watched her go before turning to look at her son.

Her *son*.

She couldn't believe it. For a long time, she and Alejandro had been content with their small family. But after all of her cousins began to pop out babies, an old longing began to fill Charity again. She hadn't felt baby fever since she was with Eric, long since coming to peace with her infertility. And then Savannah had come along, and she'd been blessed with a child that she'd never expected. She'd thought that was enough. She really did...

"What now?" Jadyn asked, still looking quite nervous.

"Well, I'm going to cook some dinner so you, me, Alejandro and Savannah can all have a meal together. But that's going to take a bit, so if you want to go back to your room or walk about, you can."

"Can I go outside?"

"You can if you stay in the yard, but I'd prefer you don't go more than a few steps away before I can show you the ropes around here. There are some gopher holes and other things that can hurt you."

"Okay... can I go into the playroom?"

"Sure! Absolutely. There are some fun games in there. I only ask that if you use any of the electronics that you don't save over any of Savannah's files. She's very attached to certain games. Everything should have plenty of memory for you to do that."

"Yeah, I can do that."

"Perfect. Go make yourself comfortable."

The boy did, pausing about halfway up the stairs. Charity waited, unsure if he was going to say anything, but in the end, he just shook his head and continued ascending. That was fine. Charity was pretty sure that he'd have lots and lots of questions in the future, but she figured he'd need time to sort out how to say them.

Not to mention building the trust to make him feel secure enough to even want to ask those trickier thoughts and worries.

So instead, she busied herself with dinner. Nothing too fancy, just some burgers, curly fries and some chicken drumsticks. She'd gotten a list of the boy's food preferences, but she didn't think a peanut butter and jelly sandwich or goldfish crackers was exactly the best meal to welcome him into their home.

She tried not to think of why the boy only had a couple of foods he liked. Part of her hoped that it was just because he was picky, but she had a pretty good idea that wasn't the reason.

"Hey there, it smells great down here."

Charity nearly jumped out of her skin, chuckling slightly when she saw it was just Alejandro coming into the kitchen.

"Did you finish up with Savannah's school work?"

"Yes. She's packing up her stuff for school on Monday and then she'll be right down." He looked around, a curious expression crossing his features.

"Where's the kid? Is he running late?"

"No, he's actually in the playroom."

"What, really? By himself?"

She nodded. "He needed some space. He seems to be fairly independent."

"Ah, I'd gotten that impression, but I do worry about him being on his lonesome."

"I don't think he's a flight risk. And if we're going to earn some of his trust, we need to give him time to process."

Alejandro closed the distance between them, draping his arm over her shoulder. "It really is incredible what you're doing here."

"What *we're* doing here," she reminded. "I wouldn't be able to do this without you."

"Hah, that's not something I hear every day."

"Are you trying to tell me that I have a hard time asking for help?"

He chuckled, shaking his head. "What? No, I would never!"

"That's right."

Charity kissed the tip of his nose, then returned back to dinner. Like usual, Alejandro set the table for her, grabbing a pitcher of ice water, iced tea, and some juice. It took her maybe another ten minutes or so, but then she was calling up to the second floor.

"Kids! It's time to eat!"

Savannah thundered down the stairs like she always did whenever there was food mentioned. At fifteen, she was somehow still growing and barely half an inch shorter than

Charity. She'd grown slightly less reedy than she'd been before, but it had been replaced with the hard, wiry muscle that came from being a kid with way too much energy and too few minutes in the day.

"What are we having?" she asked, jumping over the railing to skip the last three steps.

"Savannah! What have I told you about vaulting the stairs!?"

"That I'll end up damaging the floor and maybe myself. Sorry, Mom." She trotted over to Charity, placing a kiss on her cheek, before hurrying off to the dining room. Charity sighed, only to be surprised by Jadyn clearing his throat right above her.

"That's your kid?" he asked, still sounding suspicious.

"Yeah, that's Savannah."

"She in college?"

"Oh no, she's just fifteen. Although she did skip a grade."

"She don't look fifteen."

Charity sighed again; remember the young woman she'd first met years ago. "No, she doesn't, does she?"

Something about her answer must have satisfied Jadyn, because he came down the stairs and followed after her to the dining room. A bit later, the four of them were all arranged for their first meal as a family.

"Jadyn, we normally hold hands as we pray around the table. You don't have to if you don't want to." She wasn't sure how he was on physical touch, especially with people he didn't know that much.

He just shrugged. "I don't mind."

"Okay. Alejandro, would you mind saying the prayer?"

Her husband grinned at her, then stretched out his hands, which Savannah and Jadyn took. Charity did the same, already feeling a bit emotional.

"Dear Lord, we thank you for this food and the means with which you provided it to us. We also thank you for bringing Jadyn into our lives and ask that you help all of us be the best we can be towards each other. We are very grateful for the chance to expand our family with love and compassion."

"Amen," Charity and Savannah echoed.

"Can I pray too?" Jadyn asked.

Charity was surprised by the question, and she couldn't help the elated grin that spread across her features.

"Dear Jesus, I'm not real sure how this goes, but my Nana said that you can listen to a heart. Even though you can hear all that, I wanted to let you know, of all the families in the world, I'm real glad you had this one choose me."

Oh, *oh!* Charity's eyes misted up immediately and before she knew it, she was out of her chair.

"Jadyn, may I give you a hug?" She knelt down beside him, feeling so overwhelmed. He was such a sweet kid, a good kid. He deserved so much more than the world had given him, and she was determined to rectify that. "You can absolutely say no if you're not ready."

But instead he pushed himself out of his chair and wrapped his skinny arms around her shoulders. "Thank you," he whispered, barely loud enough to reach his ears.

"Oh honey, I'm the one who should be thanking you."

"For what?"

"For trusting us. I promise you, we won't let you down."

"Really? Cross your heart?"

Charity just hugged him harder. "Cross all of our hearts, Jadyn. If you like it here, you're stuck with us."

"I think I'd like that. I think I'd like that a lot."

24

Alejandro

"So it looks like your temperature is just fine. Can you explain to me what's going on?"

Alejandro did his best to smile warmly at Miss Watts, although his mind was on other matters. Their new son Jadyn had been in their family for about a month, and although there were plenty of learning curves for all of them, things were going fantastic.

He'd cut back his working hours for those first four weeks, but considering he was the doctor for the whole town, he couldn't exactly stay at that forever. It was only his second day, and he was running house calls, which always were a gamble.

"I'm just feeling run down, you know. A certain sort of malaise that makes it hard to get through the day."

"I see," Alejandro said, looking in his bag. He'd never done house calls in Cali but moving into a small town certainly changed how he ran his practice. "Are you feeling fatigued? Chapped lips? Any cracks in the corners of your mouth?"

"I don't know. Maybe you should examine it?"

The woman leaned forward in her kitchen chair, mouth opening slightly. Alejandro paused for a beat, the hair on the back of his neck standing up.

Was she...?

It wouldn't have been the first time that a patient had hit on him, but a lot of that had cleared up once Alejandro had gotten married. Sure, some of the single women in town had wanted a shot at the eligible new bachelor who just so happened to be a doctor, but very few of them were interested in being the mistress of the happily married town physician.

"Do you see anything concerning?" Miss Watts asked, looking up at him through her lashes.

No, she couldn't be. Alejandro was just being paranoid.

"Let me get my flashlight pen."

Grabbing the tool, he looked in the woman's mouth. No angular cheilitis, no white spots, there wasn't even any red irritation around her throat.

"Hmm, it's looking fine there. Do you have any allergies?" Alejandro stood, using a sanitation wipe to clean the light then tucking it back into his bag.

"Only an allergy to loneliness."

That was certainly a strange thing to say. Alejandro turned around only to find the woman right in front of him, her front almost touching his.

"Ma'am?"

"Surely you know what it's like, don't you? Losing your first wife and ending up married into that Miller harem."

Harem? Alejandro dubiously echoed in his mind. In what world was he in a harem? He knew that some of the townspeople weren't fond of the Millers, usually out of jealousy, but he'd never heard anything like *that.*

"I don't think that there's anything here I can help you with, but please feel free to call if you develop more symptoms."

"But doctor, I've got all the symptoms of a broken heart. Can't you tell?" She took a step forward and Alejandro took a step back, alarm flowing through him.

He was most definitely being hit on, and perhaps it shouldn't have been so out of left field to him, but his mind had been so zeroed in on growing his family that he'd forgotten about some of the more unpleasant things that happened in the world outside of the ranch.

"Look, Miss Watts, I'm not sure what you think is happening here, but I am a happily married man. I'm going to ask you to put yourself to bed while I return home to my loving family."

"You don't have to be noble for me. Certainly, a strong, intelligent man such as yourself has needs. Needs that can't be met by a farm girl and her backwater family."

"Miss *Watts!*" Alejandro wasn't exactly the most confrontational person, but he wasn't about to let some woman insult his beloved wife.

"Come on now. We're both adults here, aren't we?"

Part of Alejandro wanted to push the woman away and just run for it, but he was also well aware of the accusations an unscrupulous person could levy against someone they wanted to punish for rejecting them.

"You know what, why don't I call her now?"

"What?"

Alejandro pulled his phone out and hit the speed dial,

praying Charity would answer. And thankfully she did, her voice sounding over the speaker.

"Hey, what's up?"

"Oh, just wanted to check in, honey. And tell you that I love you."

"Aw, isn't that as sweet as pie. I love you too."

Miss Watt's expression quickly faded from shock to irritation, but Alejandro couldn't care less. "And how's our son doing?"

"Um, he's alright. I showed him the pond and he's been trying to learn how to swim with Savannah. I'm sitting on the shore, keeping an eye on it all."

Word by word, Miss Watts began to deflate. Alejandro took that as his chance to leave, so he muted the call quickly.

"Thanks for your time. You do right by yourself, Miss Watts."

She let out a huff then flounced off deeper into her house. Alejandro took that as his cue and hurried out, taking Charity off mute.

"So, you wanna tell me what really was going on there?" she asked. Because of course his wife knew something was up. She was far too perceptive for her own good. Either that or she could read him like a book.

"Just had a patient who was crossing one line too many."

"Ah, another house call turned soap opera?"

"Something like that."

"You haven't had one of those in a while."

"Yeah, most of this town is pretty well-behaved."

"We're lucky. From what I hear from my cousins up in Montana, they've got some real meanies." She paused a moment, her voice going soft. "But you're okay, right?"

Alejandro got into his car and quickly started in the direction of home. "Yeah. I just can't wait to see you again."

She chuckled lightly, a soft, pretty sound that never failed to make him incredibly grateful that their paths had crossed.

"But you just saw me this morning."

"I know, but it wasn't enough."

"Oh really now? Guess you need a refill."

"I most certainly do," Alejandro said, grinning like a loon. "I think about five kisses and a dozen hugs will be a good start."

"Wow, you've got it down to a numerical prescription, huh?"

"Well, it is a part of my job."

She laughed again, the perfect balm to his stressful day. They continued to banter back and forth on speakerphone the entire way home, and when he arrived, she was waiting there on the porch.

Putting his car into park, he strode right up to her, taking her in his arms and giving her a thorough kiss. When they parted, he rested his forehead against hers.

"Welcome home, darling," Charity said, her cheeks flushed in that adorable way of hers.

"Happy to be here," he answered before kissing her again.

And he meant it.

Oh boy, did he mean it.

25

Savannah

Savannah strode through the school hallway, heading for the lunchroom with determination. As a junior, it was actually nowhere near her meal period, but she was on a most urgent mission.

Her little brother hadn't been with the family long, just three short months, but Savannah took her big sister duties quite seriously. She'd been an only child for most of her life and she'd largely been fine with it, but now that she had a little sibling and a mom, she was fiercely protective of her found family.

So, when she'd heard a younger student talking smack about her little brother, she'd confronted them. They'd clearly been intimidated by an upperclassman with over a foot on them and had spilled the beans to her that it was none other than Stacy

Kellmen and Patrick Deerly who had started some of the worst rumors.

And she just couldn't abide by that.

Her little brother had been through a lot, even more than her, and although she didn't know all of it, Savannah wanted to turn things around for him. So she couldn't stand idly by and let people terrorize or besmirch Jadyn. No, she was going to do something about it.

Part of her wondered why her little brother hadn't told her. She got not telling the adults because sometimes adults just didn't get things. But she was a high schooler too. If anyone was going to understand just how confusing and tricky the politics of a school were, it was her.

Savannah supposed it was reasonable to assume that he just didn't trust her that much yet, but she didn't understand why. Everyone knew that she told the truth to a fault, sometimes saying things that other people would cover up with a white lie. It wasn't that she went out of her way to hurt anyone or be rude, but she also believed her friends and loved ones deserved her genuine opinions. Not fluffed up ones.

Oh well, she could give him a little grace. Her mother had told her that he wasn't exactly the most trusting individual, and they'd have to be patient. So, Savannah would be patient. It was the least that she could do considering the kid handled her... quirks relatively well.

As she grew older, Savannah began to understand more and more that she really wasn't like a lot of the kids around her. Her brain worked in a different way, and she perceived things... alternatively. It could be unsettling to some, but Jadyn rolled with it as easy as any of the other surprises in his life.

Finally, she reached the cafeteria and pushed the door open.

She had a vague idea of what Stacy and Patrick looked like, but she was kind of counting on her status as a junior to convince people to point them out.

Approaching the closest table, she tapped on the corner. That was enough to get the middle schoolers looking up at her in surprise.

"Hey, I'm looking for Stacy and Patrick."

"Which Stacy?"

"Kellmen."

They pointed to a table at the far side and Savannah strode towards them.

"What are you doing here?"

The fervent whisper had Savannah frozen mid-step, and she looked beside her to see Jadyn sitting with a horrified expression on his face.

"Big sister stuff," she answered resolutely before continuing her march forward. It didn't take her long to reach Stacy's table, and she stood right across from the girl. The conversation faded fast, leaving an unnatural sort of quiet for a middle school cafeteria.

"Uh... hello?"

"Hey there, Stacy. I've heard you've got an awful lot of opinions about my little brother, so I'm gonna ask you to stop with all that."

She huffed. "I don't know what you're talking about."

"Oh, you don't?" Savannah tapped on the kid's shoulder closest to her and he quickly vacated, allowing her to sit. She had no intention of hurting anyone or getting into a fight with kids, but she had no problem with them maybe thinking she might. "That's strange, because I've heard from a couple of people that you've been saying all sorts of nasty things about my little brother."

"He's not actually your brother," she snapped, rolling her eyes. "You, like, just met him."

"See, that's where you're wrong. Look, I get that you're young, but you're also two years older than my brother, so you can see why I have an issue with an older kid picking on him.

"You should know better, cause you're plenty smart, so why don't we just nip this in the bud and all move on?"

"Whatever." God bless the middle school compunction to appear effortlessly cool by pretending to be unaffected by anything. "You're a freak too. My big brother says you're about the most annoying person he's ever met."

"Your brother?" Savannah mused, resting her chin in her hand. "You mean Brent? Ah, that explains things." Perhaps her chuckle was a little dryer than it needed to be, but goodness, the Kellmen siblings really did take after one another, didn't they?

"What do you mean?"

"Brent is a mediocre football player with not quite mediocre grades who most likely will never amount to anything if he doesn't learn to take personal responsibility. He likes to bully others that he's jealous of, and he hates that he's not quite good enough with wordplay to ever go toe to toe with me." Charity had taught Savannah to be nice, and that intelligence was on a scale so she shouldn't look down on other people who had a different sort of smarts than her. But sometimes it was just so *easy* to insult folks where it hurt. Especially if they were meanies.

Did that make Savannah a bully too? She wasn't sure. All she knew was that her gut was roiling at how unrepentant the girl was about tormenting her brother. Savannah wasn't even going to repeat the things she'd heard.

"Pfffft, okay," Stacy said.

"You don't know what half of those words mean, do you?" Savannah asked.

"W-w-we're sorry," the boy sputtered beside her. "We didn't mean it!"

Savannah grinned and looked at the young man. "And you must be Patrick."

"Y-yeah."

"Alright, Patrick, I accept your apology, but I'm gonna need you to do something for me."

He looked downright horrified. "W-what's that?"

"Look, I'll admit my brother hasn't had it easy. A lot of people have been *real* mean to him. If y'all could use all that popular middle school power of yours and spread some *nice* rumors, I'd be much obliged."

"You want us to spread... nice rumors?"

"Yeah! Like that he's really funny. Or that although he's quiet, he's a great listener. He also does some pretty hilarious impressions."

Patrick was looking at her like she was some sort of monster come to crush him, but at least he nodded. "Uh, okay. I can do that."

"This is *so* stupid," Stacy spat. "Your whole family is full of hermit freaks!"

"Ah, hermit. You know that's not an insult, right? And being introverted isn't exactly a character flaw." Savannah fixed her gaze back on Stacy. "Look, I proposed what I think is a pretty reasonable agreement. Why are you so set on tormenting my brother?"

The girl didn't answer, but that was probably because a hand landed on Savannah's shoulder. Looking up, she saw none other than Brent.

Ah. There definitely was a downside to having the high school attached to the middle school by a hallway and wide set of stairs. Savannah had thought it was really bizarre when she first moved, but now she understood it was just a necessity of small-town life.

"What are you doing talking to my sister?"

"Brent, I'm glad you could join us! Your sister has been bullying my little brother, so I figured we'd have a talk and hopefully see eye to eye."

"Maybe your little brother deserves it."

Savannah gave him a bored look too. "Really, that's what we're going with? My ten-year-old brother deserves to be bullied?"

"What's a matter? Can't dry his tears with all your money?"

Savannah rolled her eyes. "Is that what this is about? Are you mad that my parents are affluent? And you've chosen to express your jealousy by making up hateful rumors about my brother?"

"He's not even your brother!"

Savannah jumped up, turning so she was face-to-face with the boy. Well, almost face-to-face, he had a couple of inches on her.

"Yes. He. Is."

"Pffft, no he ain't, and that Miller lady ain't your real mom either. Your dad just married her for her money!"

Those were fighting words, but Savannah kept her fists at her sides. She could sense Jadyn watching her very astutely and wanted to set a good example. Besides, Charity had always taught her to try to avoid physical confrontations. Buuuuut... she'd also said that sometimes a fist did better than a dictionary.

"I realize you're saying that to get a rise out of me, but it would most likely be much more effective if my father wasn't already a wealthy doctor on his own." Brent opened his mouth like he was going to interrupt her, but Savannah kept on. "Look, I understand that I'm stupidly lucky, and there are a lot of people who will never have the resources that I just happened to be born into. But that doesn't mean you get to take it out on my little brother, got it?

"Because, lemme tell ya, if the only way you can think of to right the injustices in the world is to pick on a ten-year-old kid, you're making a real statement about your character."

"Whatever, freakin' aspie."

"Oh nooo, an insult about my mind now. Look, I'm sorry that you have the comprehension skills of a particularly moldy potato, but that's not my fault. Maybe if you put your energy into actually studying instead of trash-talking my family, you wouldn't have a GPA of 2!"

It was a low blow, but Savannah's anger was simmering even hotter just below the surface. The whole situation should have been easy! Why Brent and his sister were being so insistent on harassing a little kid who was dealing with a whole lot of trauma and the stress that came from trying to forge a new family, she didn't understand. It was so much wasted time and energy just to hurt someone who didn't deserve to be hurt!

"Shut up!"

It happened fast. One moment the two of them were face-to-face, tension thick enough to cut with a knife; the next Brent pulled his fist back and aimed it straight at her face.

Savannah tried to duck, she did, but he still managed a glancing blow that skipped across the side of her cheek. It hurt something fierce, but suddenly the anger in her went from simmering to an outright inferno.

"Are you kidding me?" she snapped, baring her teeth while holding her face.

"Leave her alone!"

Something slammed into Brent, knocking him a few steps, and it took Savannah a beat to realize that it was Jadyn! The kid had launched himself off the table and was on the larger student's back, punching at his head.

"Wait, Jadyn! No!"

Brent let out a stream of curses and tried to reach behind him, hands curled like he was ready to hurt.

"Don't touch him!" Savannah grabbed Brent's wrist, jerking him away, but he just shoved her into a table. She toppled over but managed to spring back on her feet, grabbing the back of Jadyn's shirt and pulling him off of the jock. He went with her, thankfully, and she managed to set him on the ground just as Brent kicked her in the back.

"Stop it!" she yelled.

Jadyn tried to launch himself at Brent again, but Savannah caught him in midair. "Would the two of you stop it!?"

But then the jock tried to swing on her, so she kicked out, catching him right in the crotch. It was what some people would call a low blow, but she wasn't sure what she was supposed to do given the situation. Her arms were full of her little brother and apparently, she was in the first physical fight of her high school career.

Savannah's heart was pumping in her chest, and she was reminded of the first time she'd seen Charity get into a brawl at a fall festival. It had certainly been exciting at the time and had definitely contributed to how much Savannah had been enamored by her new mother.

"Hey, what's going on here?!"

Savannah froze, looking at what had to be a teacher who was staring them down like they were evil incarnate.

"Uh-oh."

Savannah's leg bounced as she waited for Charity to arrive. Thankfully her father was at work, but that was only a slight comfort considering that her mother would most definitely tell him that she'd gotten in trouble at school.

It was the first time she'd ever been reprimanded for anything that wasn't correcting a teacher too much, so she was a little out of her depth. As for Jadyn, he was sitting stoically beside her, staring straight ahead as if he was daring anyone to say anything to him.

He was braver than her, that was for sure, but then again, he'd probably gone through a whole lot worse.

Finally, Charity came in, giving them a curious look. They didn't have time to talk before the principal stepped out and motioned for all of them to come in.

"So what's going on here? I was told there was an incident?"

"Yes, your daughter got into a physical altercation with another student, and then your son jumped in."

Charity's eyebrows went nearly up to her hairline. "Is that true?"

"Brent swung at me. I tried to dodge, but I didn't do it in time, and Jadyn tried to protect me."

A myriad of emotions passed across her mother's face, and she looked to Jadyn. "You protected your big sister?"

He gave a singular solid nod. "He hit her."

"Mrs. Miller—"

"Lumis-Miller," Charity corrected quickly.

"Mrs. Lumis-Miller," he tried again. "We have a zero-toler-ance policy here, so we're going to have to send your kids home for the day and give Savannah another day of in-school suspension."

"No."

"No?" the principal repeated like she'd just started speaking in tongues.

"No. This is both of my children's first infractions, and they didn't start the fight—they just finished it. I'll take them home for today, and even keep them home tomorrow, but on Monday they will be returning to school without so much as a blemish on their record."

"With all due respect, you can't just order this away."

"Oh, I'm not ordering it any which way. I'm just telling you what's going to happen. You see, my children were forced to defend themselves because none of your teachers were on the ball. What, are children just left alone to do whatever they want?

"Not to mention my youngest is just coming out of a big tran-sition and several of his needs are in his school file. Not only have those been ignored, but his health has been put on the line. I'm sure his caseworker wouldn't be thrilled to hear how this school is treating one of her former charges."

The principal swallowed hard. Charity had taught Savannah a million and one times that it was wrong for them to abuse their money or societal position, but it was kind of cool to see her mother's sharper side come out.

"Right. A day and a half of out-of-school suspension then, but it doesn't go on their records."

"Perfect. And don't worry, I'll have a long talk with my children about keeping their hands to themselves. But do make sure the other participants also understand that I do give both of my kids permission to defend themselves, and if my daughter comes home with another bruise on her face, I will be getting lawyers involved."

"Right. Of course. I'll make sure they understand."

"Alright, let's go home and discuss your punishments," Charity said, standing up. Wordlessly Savannah and Jadyn followed after her.

Technically, Savannah knew there was probably a better way she could have gone about the whole situation, but it wasn't like there was a manual. Maybe if she'd been raised with a little sibling, she wouldn't be so lost, but she only had about three months' experience.

They continued to say nothing as they got into Mom's extended cab truck and headed towards home. But instead of taking the left-hand turn that would lead them out of town and to the ranch, Charity turned right.

Maybe she wanted to pick something up. Or worse, maybe she was going to stop at Dad's office. That idea made Savannah squirm in her seat. It was no secret that her father was the slightly softer of her parents, but goodness, he would look at her with such disappointment that it would make her heart wither. He worked so hard and was *such* a good dad despite losing Savannah's biological mom young; the thought of letting him down was borderline unbearable.

But they didn't go to Dad's office. Instead, they stopped in front of the specialty ice cream parlor that had opened right next to Uncle Baz's mechanic shop.

"What's going on?" Savannah asked, saying what Jadyn wouldn't.

"Let's go inside." They followed her yet again, but as they went through the door, Jadyn's hand slipped into Savannah's.

Oh!

Savannah didn't say anything, her steps sputtering only a moment. While she'd been trying to bond with her little brother ever since he'd arrived, she understood that he wasn't the most physically affectionate person. While Savannah loved hugs, high fives, kisses on the cheeks and just about everything else, Jadyn seemed to prefer having a personal bubble.

So yeah, it was a pretty big moment. Even if they were in trouble, she was doing something right.

"Okay, the two of you can get whatever you want."

"What?" Jadyn asked, voice sharp.

"Don't worry, it's not a trick. I want both of you to get a nice treat. Whatever you want. And don't worry about ruining dinner. Clara already messaged me that she needed to push it back by an hour. Something about a diva at her place."

"So, we're not in trouble?" Savannah asked cautiously.

"No, you're not in trouble. We do need to have a talk about some things, and I want you to tell me everything that happened in detail, but you'll never be in trouble for protecting family."

Charity crouched, carefully placing a hand on Jadyn's shoulder. When he didn't flinch, she let it stay there.

"I am so proud of you for helping your big sister in what must have been a scary situation. Thank you so much, Jadyn. You have no idea how much that means to me."

"I..." Jadyn looked like he was going to cry, and Savannah wished she could just crush him into a hug. Instead, she just squeezed his hand. "He was hurting her."

"Exactly. We don't use our fists unless we absolutely have to, but when it comes to protecting family, you do what you gotta do.

And if you get in trouble for it, I'll be right there to protect you too."

She stood up, letting out a warbling breath. Charity didn't cry too often, but Savannah got the feeling she might be about to. "Don't get me wrong, if you misbehave, if you break a rule, you will have to face the consequences. But I'll never punish my children for standing up for themselves. Ever. Does that make sense?"

Jadyn nodded, and in a moment Savannah never would have predicted, he reached his other hand out to Charity. Her bottom lip trembled in what Savannah instantly recognized as her mother's happy cry, but she managed to reach out and take her son's hand without bursting into tears.

"Ready to go look at the menu?"

Jadyn nodded. "Will you help me read it?"

"Of course. Whatever you need."

26

Cassidy

"Ten!"

Cassidy sank onto her rear end, legs shaking borderline violently from exertion. Patting the ground next to her, she grabbed her towel and wiped her dripping face.

Funny, to think that there had once been a time where she was dissatisfied with how hard Alejandro was pushing her. But after two years with him, she'd finally graduated from his treatment, and he recommended her to another PT in the city with a full facility that was made for her level of care.

No longer did she have to work on things like being able to hold her cup of coffee for more than five minutes or being able to stand up without being lightheaded. Instead, she was moving on to being able to walk quickly, or balance on one leg as long as she could. Also, her flexibility. Cassidy had no idea how much she'd lost in the wheelchair and while she was learning to walk again. It used to be that she could rest her palms on the floor when she bent over, but now her fingertips hovered at least an inch or two above the ground.

"How we doing over here?"

Cassidy looked up at her physical therapist, a fairly jacked fellow named Phil. He was nice enough, even though sometimes his optimism felt a little forced to her. But maybe that was just her crankiness. Even with all she'd accomplished, Cassidy knew she still sometimes struggled with feeling frazzled quickly.

"I finished up my last set of reps."

"Very good! Do you want to do another round of flexibility exercises?"

Cassidy gave it genuine thought for a moment. There had also been a time where she would push herself and push herself until she vomited or fell over, but she'd found a sort of balance since then. She could keep going, yeah, she was physically capable, but there was a line she could pass where she would do more damage than good, hurting her muscles instead of strengthening them.

"No, I think I'm good for now."

"Really? That's awesome. You know, I was a bit skeptical when you first joined us over here a couple months back."

"What do you mean?"

"Well, your file warned that you were a real Type A, to the point of damaging yourself. Normally I don't want to work with people who will undo all the work we put in together, but Dr. Lumis vouched for you. He said you'd improved on the habit a lot, so I decided to take a chance. Turns out he was right."

Perhaps it was a strange thing to be pleased about, but Cassidy's pride bubbled up. "Thanks, Phil."

"No problem. You head home and rest up now. I'll see you on Wednesday?"

"I'll be here."

"Great. We'll work on more of your arms and shoulders."

Cassidy nodded, then went about her normal routine of leaving. First going to the restroom, washing her face and hands, then sitting in the lobby for about ten minutes while she caught her breath. Then it was grabbing her walker from the receptionist and heading out to her car.

Now there was a definite improvement in her life. When Charity had found someone who could modify her old truck so she could drive it with her hands, Cassidy had been thrilled. He'd done the alterations lickety-split.

And that had been the day she discovered she was too terrified to get into the driver's side. She tried, oh boy had she tried, but the moment she was in the seat, she started shaking too hard to even put the key in the ignition.

So yeah, that had been fun. It had taken about a year of very specific therapy on top of her regular stuff to get her to be able to even sit in the truck and turn it on, but she'd been progressing from there until she was pretty much able to drive herself anywhere within a two-hour radius. Past that was iffy, as she'd start to feel exhausted and jittery, but the amount of freedom it gave her was definitely nice.

She no longer had to depend on everyone else for rides. Not that anyone had ever begrudged her, but it had been strangely infantilizing. Now, if she wanted to go to the town store and grab herself a soda they didn't have, she could do that. She could head to her PT without worrying about interfering with anybody else's schedules. It was easier, that was for sure.

Heading home, she drove without incident, happily

humming along to the low tones over her radio. She couldn't play it loud like she used to because it was too much stimulation and noise, but she could listen to it quietly. It was a compromise, and one she could live with.

She arrived at her destination without anything of note happening, and that was plenty fine with her. Switching to her cane, she headed inside the main house to see Mick standing at the kitchen island, a full meal laid out while he checked something on his phone. He looked handsome there, bathed in the light of the just-setting sun, and Cassidy couldn't help but feel so incredibly lucky.

They'd wanted to move out on their own after they were married. Make a house just like Charity and Alejandro had on the other edge of the property, and that would be that. But after seeing how long it had taken the eldest Miller daughter to get that taken care of and knowing that theirs would take twice that time because of all the accessibility measures, she'd opted to stay in the main house with Papa for a few more years. It wasn't like they were tight on room, considering that Charity and Clara had both moved out.

Sure, they were still just engaged, with another eight months until their wedding, and Mick was still living in his RV, but it was nice to know what their plans would be once everything was all settled out.

"Hey there," Cassidy said, thumping over to him. Her body was incredibly sore and exhausted, but not so drawn out that she couldn't kiss her handsome future husband.

"Hey," he answered, setting down his phone and returning her kiss. "How'd your day go?"

"Great! I finished all of the exercises my PT gave me, and I stopped of my own accord."

"Really?"

"He offered me to do some more sets, but I realized my body had hit its limit so I called it for the day."

"Wow, I'm proud of you." He leaned down again, giving her another sweet kiss. Cassidy couldn't help but grin, her whole-body filling with bubbling happiness. "Are you hungry?"

"Definitely. This all looks so good!"

"Thanks, I've been working on and off with Clara when she's around."

Cassidy beamed at her fiancé. Although she probably wasn't going to say it out loud, at least not at the moment. She didn't want to get weepy and sappy over a meal that her fiancé had gone through so much trouble to make her. But the handsome man inspired her so much. He'd been given nothing in his life, had worked hard for every single crumb of good. And that's why she was working so hard to be able to dance with him at their wedding.

After all, it was good to have goals, right?

27

Mick

ick wasn't really the crying type, but he'd be lying if he didn't admit his eyes got a little watery a couple of times throughout his wedding.

And how could he not shed a tear or two? Seeing all of their family and friends surrounding them made him feel soft and squishy inside. There had been a time, not that long ago, where his side of the church would have been completely empty. But since moving to the Miller's, he'd made his own bonds along the way. Naturally there were all the sisters and the one brother besides Cassidy, then their significant others, then those significant other's family members if they had them. And there were the seasonal ranch hands they hired occasionally for special projects, and some other horse riders he met at the rodeo through Daisy.

Yeah, Mick wasn't really a lone soul anymore, but that was just fine with him.

Of course, it wasn't just seeing their friends around him. It was also the moment that he first saw his bride. The doors opened and there was Cassidy, dressed in white with her walker done up in pretty ribbons where it was safe. She walked forward, Papa Miller right beside her, and Mick was still not quite sure how he managed not to burst into tears right then and there.

She looked *beautiful*.

She'd started to grow her hair out in the past year, and it was done up in intricate curls atop her head. Her dress was exquisite, and it fit her figure just right. Granted, what else could be expected from Clara's top-notch tailoring? Mick didn't know the technical details of the dress, but he didn't need to. But he *did* know that he was going to remember that moment for the rest of his life.

It was a lot of emotions to go through, that was for sure, and by the time the reception rolled around, Mick was plenty ready for some dancing, laughing, and eating. Anything that didn't involve his eyes stinging with unshed tears. It wasn't that he resented his emotions, but they were exhausting, and he could use a break.

There were speeches still, but those weren't too bad, and then Mick was finally getting some food in his belly. He probably should have snacked on something beforehand, but that morning his stomach had been too unsettled for any sort of matter to be put into it.

There was lots of laughing, as well as interrupted bites as people approached them to talk. Mick didn't mind; it wasn't like he was in a rush. As far as he was concerned, the day could last just about forever, and he'd be happy.

Until the DJ started talking.

Mick had been so into the conversation he was having with Mrs. Jeanette that he was startled when the man's voice first came over the speakers. He went through the normal stuff that one would expect, but then he started going into unscripted territory.

"And if I could have the groom come to the dance floor?"

Mick blinked, looking around as if someone had answers for him. But Cassidy was still in the bathroom and no one else seemed to think it was strange. Frowning, Mick stood and slowly walked to the center of the floor.

"Perfect. Everyone clap for the lucky man who got to marry the love of his life today!"

Mick chuckled good-naturedly. He didn't mind anyone pointing out he was incredibly fortunate. As long as anyone didn't make those awful jokes about him being forced to marry someone, or act like being with Cassidy was going to end his life, he was fairly chill.

"These two have quite the love story. If you don't know it, you should go ahead and ask 'em sometime. But not right now, because right now, we're about to have the first dance with the bride and groom!"

Oh no. Mick went pale and tried to make a stopping motion by his neck. Cassidy and Mick had agreed on skipping all of the usual dance traditions, not wanting to put so much pressure on Cassidy. If her chair accidentally rolled across someone's foot, it could be a pretty serious injury, and she was definitely using her chair for the reception.

"Hey, uh—"

"And here's the beautiful bride now!"

Mick looked in the direction that the DJ was pointing to see Cassidy sitting in the doorway. Her dress had changed, no longer the floor-length, white gown and instead a knee-length ivory one. It showed off her strong arms and striking shoulders, leaving Mick even more scrambled than he was before.

Clearly, she'd planned something, but Mick was certainly out of the loop.

Like something out of a movie, she rolled closer to him, right up to the edge of the dance floor. When she came to a stop she took a deep breath, then *stood*.

It wasn't the first time he'd seen her stand, sure. But it was the first time she'd done it completely unaided, in a dress and sparkling flats, in front of an audience. Without so much as a waver, she stepped closer with her hand raised.

"Would you like to dance?" she murmured, eyes filled with so much love that it made his heart ache.

"Is this really happening?" he answered, taking her hand in his.

"Just follow my lead." She winked at him as slow, beautiful music filled the hall. Mick could sense that everyone's eyes were on him, but for once, he didn't mind. Cassidy deserved to be in the spotlight, and he was just lucky enough to be in her orbit.

"Here we go."

And then she was indeed leading him across the floor in a simple waltz. Mick wasn't really used to being on the following side of things, but it was plenty easy to go along. And if that was what Cassidy needed to dance with him without a mobility aid, well he'd be happy doing it for the rest of his life.

Because his wife was glorious, truly glorious, practically glowing with pride and love. It made him feel blessed, truly blessed, that she had chosen him out of everyone. They'd been through a lot together, just the two of them. She understood his needs as a type 1 diabetic, and he helped her with whatever she needed on her own healing journey. Despite being from two different walks of life, they were two peas in a pod.

"I love you," Cassidy murmured as they floated across the ground.

"I love you too," Mick answered.

He meant it. He meant it even more than the words themselves implied. His heart felt full to bursting, and those tears he'd been avoiding had finally made their escape to fall in earnest. He was in another world at the moment, one where only he and Cassidy existed, lost in their love.

When the dance finally ended, Mick kissed Cassidy for all he was worth. A cheer came up from all around them, but Mick hardly noticed.

"You're incredible," he whispered, afraid he'd break into sobs if he spoke much louder.

"*We're* incredible," she countered, wrapping her arms tightly around him. "And we just keep on improving. Together."

"Together," Mick agreed.

And they had the rest of their lives to keep on climbing.

28

Clara

"And you're sure you're alright coming with me?"

Although Clara was concentrating on the road, she could still sense the slightly perturbed look Nathan gave her.

"Clara, that's the fifth time you've asked since this morning."

"Well, I just wanted to be sure."

He reached over, his scarred hand comforting as it rested atop hers. "I'm fine. And I'm excited to find out what we're having."

Clara nodded, looking down at her slightly rounder stomach. Despite being engaged the third of all her sisters, she was actually the first to be married. She guessed she and Nathan moved fast, at least compared to Papa, who dated Jeanette for over three years before proposing. But they hadn't needed to wait for an entire house to be built, nor did they have to worry about recovering from traumatic car accidents. Nathan had his own homestead that Clara was more than happy to work on with him, and it was small enough scale that she could still spend plenty of time doing her chores at the Miller Ranch. She usually switched every other day with Sunday as her day of rest, and Cici picked up whatever slack was caused by her absence.

"Part of me has a hard time believing this is real," she murmured, her emotions surging within her. After so long daydreaming about Prince Charmings and romantic movies, she really did have her happy ending. Except it wasn't a happy ending so much as it was a happy new beginning.

"I know what you mean," Nathan said, grinning dopily over at her.

And goodness, if she didn't just love that expression to pieces. Her husband had continued to work on himself just like he promised, improving day by day. Most of the time, his walls were down, and she felt privileged that she got to see such unguarded parts of him. But he still had a tendency to push himself too much, to force himself to be strong, which was why she couldn't help but be a little worried about him going to the hospital for her ultrasound with her.

It wasn't like he was phobic, not at all, but considering his lengthy hospital stays, it wasn't like she could blame him for wanting to avoid the place.

At least they were going to the obstetrics wing. That small blessing would hopefully help the memory be a happy one, and not a borderline horror one.

There was quite a line to get into the parking garage, as usual, but eventually they did get a spot and headed towards their entrance. Clara's pregnancy hadn't affected her too much yet, so she was able to stride along easily, although she had made the switch to flats instead of her wedges.

Once they were inside, there was the usual rigamarole of getting checked in, then sitting and waiting to be shown into a private room, then sitting and waiting for an ultrasound tech. It was a largely boring process, and it was only exacerbated by the nervous energy inside of Clara.

She was the first Miller sibling in her chunk of the family to have a biological child, so that was pretty daunting. She knew in most families there was at least a mom to explain all the mundane things that never made it into movies or books, but the New Mexico Millers didn't have that luxury. Not for the first time, the sharp, biting knife of loss stabbed at Clara. She really did miss her mom.

It had been over a decade, sure, but a lot had happened in the past couple of years that rehashed the melancholy of having a parent that passed. Clara's wedding, finding out she was pregnant, Nathan going a year without any readmittance to the hospital... all of those would have been nice to have her mother celebrate. But that wasn't her fate in life, so she would just have to settle for the faint feeling of her mother's presence.

Thankfully, the tech didn't make her wait over an hour in the cold room. About fifteen minutes later, he was marching right in, a kind grin on his features.

"Hello there, are we ready to find out if you're having a little boy or a little girl?"

Clara nodded eagerly while Nathan spoke beside her. "We're just happy as long as they're healthy."

"I just want to know what kind of little outfits to make them," Clara added. Granted, she could make her baby boy the frilliest, pinkest dress and he wouldn't know it from a potato, but she also knew that dressing them up in adorable clothes was mostly for her benefit, not theirs. She was *just* practical enough to know that her baby would most likely prefer being naked over everything else, but they could compromise with her once a week or so. Or at least that's what she hoped. Her cousin-in-law, Leilani, just had twins a few months ago, and from what Clara heard, they were quite vocal about their hate of any sort of clothing in general.

Oh well, at least she wasn't going to have to deal with that. As far as she knew, twins hadn't been in the Miller genealogy in at least three generations. Leilani's pair must have come from her own family, especially since it was a maternally carried sort of inclination.

"So, I know this is your first pregnancy, so I'm going to explain everything step-by-step before we do it. Please, ask any and all questions you have, even if they seem like common sense to you. Anything I can do to assuage you, I'm game for."

Clara nodded and the tech went to the corner, uncovering a machine and rolling it over to her. With the patience of a saint, he explained the wand, the monitor, and pretty much everything else. She could tell he was trying to have some fun with it, making a joke here, a terrible pun there. And although Clara wasn't exactly in the most effervescent mood, she still appreciated his charm.

"Alright, are you ready?"

Clara nodded, laying back on the table. The tech arranged the blanket around her and lifted her gown to tuck it over her belly. Although Clara hadn't been thin to start with, she could just begin to see the rounding of her soft belly. Part of her worried that her baby wasn't big enough, that she needed to get it more nutrients that she just wasn't providing.

"Okay, just a little reminder, this gel is gonna be cold, okay?"

Another nod, and then he was smearing it onto her belly. It wasn't quite the texture she expected, and he pressed a lot harder with the wand than she'd anticipated. Huh.

But then she saw it, a strange sliver of silver and white.

"Is that my baby?" Clara asked, Nathan practically leaning over her.

"Um..."

Clara's brows went up. "Um?"

"Sorry, just figuring out if that was an arm or a leg." The tech smiled brightly at her. "But looks like that's an arm! Nice and chunky, the way we like to see them."

Clara heaved a sigh of relief; his tone had her really worried for a moment. The tech pointed out a couple of things but seemed distracted by something, like he had something exciting to get back to. Clara tried not to feel salty about it, but when he hurriedly dismissed himself, she couldn't help but feel a little put off.

But then the doctor was coming in *with* the tech.

"Hey, I just wanted to show Dr. Hernandez herself your ultrasound."

"Why?" Clara asked, suspicion rising again.

"I asked, actually," Dr. Hernandez said with a grin like that answered anything. "Javier here was just saying that he wasn't sure if he saw a leg or an arm at first, which is some pretty advanced development."

The tech sat down again and wordlessly showed the doctor things, pointing a couple of places, and the doctor nodded.

"Goodness, Clara, it's clear that both of your genes are very strong. Are you sure you're only sixteen weeks along?"

"That's our best guess from when I missed my first period."

The doctor let out a low whistle. "Well, this is a good sign.

Normally twins can be very undersized, but it seems yours are doing just fine."

"That's great. Wait, what!?"

That was Nathan. Clara was too stunned to say anything for a moment. "Did... did you just say that we are having twins?"

"Yes indeed, it does look that way. Congratulations on your little girls!"

Clara couldn't think, could hardly breathe, and she looked to Nathan in surprise.

"I thought you said that twins didn't run in your family?" he said, looking like he didn't know whether to grin or cry. Clara was right in the same boat with him.

"I didn't think they did!"

"Well, there's always a first for everything," Dr. Hernandez said. "Now, considering how large your babies already are, I do want to schedule some tests for gestational diabetes and also discuss backup plans in case a natural birth isn't possible."

"You think I'm going to need a c-section?" Clara asked, her mind automatically going to the worst.

"The hope is no, but it's good to be prepared. We won't really know until we get a little closer, but it is more common with twins."

"O-okay," Clara said, her mind spinning. She was going to have twins. Two babies. Two little girl babies to love and adore.

"Don't worry," Nathan said, gripping her hands in his. "Now we have double the kids to love."

Thank goodness for him. His presence was grounding to her, and the shock began to ebb ever so slightly.

"You're not upset?"

"Upset? How could I be? Surprised, sure. But we wanted to

build a family together, and while I thought we might have a little more time, I'm not upset about speedrunning it a bit."

Clara wasn't quite sure if she let out a little laugh or a cry, but a strangled sound left her throat before she leaned forward and kissed him.

"I love you."

"I love you too, and I'll love our double mint twins too." He kissed her another time, and then once more before the doctor cleared her throat. "You're going to be an excellent mother, Clara. I know it."

His words filled Clara with far more certainty than she probably had any right to. She'd always wanted a big family, so yeah, maybe it wasn't such a bad thing to get a head start. Because as long as she had her family, she knew she could get through anything.

29

Nathan

athan hurried through his kitchen, putting a kettle on to boil and grabbing Clara's specially blended tea her father had concocted. The sound of his wife losing her lunch and probably her breakfast was a rather morbid background track to his ministrations, but it encouraged him to go faster.

While the water boiled, he quickly snagged Clara's medicine, a sports drink and a straw while he was at it. The first part of her pregnancy had been so easy despite having twins, but things had taken a sudden terrible turn in week eighteen.

Hyperemesis Gravidarum was supposed to set in around week six or eight, but Clara's had set in during week eighteen. And it was also supposed to resolve itself around week twenty, but nope, Clara's was still going strong.

Nathan had heard of morning sickness, sure, but he didn't

know that there was a type that was so strong and pervasive that it could be lethal if not treated. Clara could hardly keep anything down some days, relying on tea, sports drinks, and meal replacement shakes just to get by. She'd been hospitalized twice to get an IV into her, and Nathan was resolved to make sure she didn't have to make another trip until her next appointment.

"I'll be just another minute!" he called, pouring the hot water into the little steeping thing that he put the loose-leaf mix Papa Miller had made into. He'd never known there was so much ceremony to tea until he'd ended up with the middle Miller daughter.

Adding some lavender honey and a tiny splash of heavy cream in it for calories, Nathan headed up the stairs as fast as he could without spilling. His mobility really had increased since his first grafts, and his dizzy spells were few and far between. It still was quite easy to become overheated, and he had to avoid sunburn studiously or he was likely to both scald himself and get sick, but other than that his health had greatly improved since he'd first met Clara.

He gave most of the credit to her. Because of her, he'd gone to therapy, and he also started eating better. No more relying on cup of noodles and whatever he could drag up enough energy to heat. He had protein, veggies, fruits, pretty much anything he could ask for. Although he didn't like to depend on Clara's wealth very much, he certainly enjoyed that she didn't count pennies in the kitchen.

"Mrrphggg..."

Nathan wasn't quite sure what his wife said, but he could hear her misery even from where she was inside their upstairs bathroom. Poor thing. His heart ached for her, and he finally understood a wee little bit of how she felt whenever he was struggling with his health.

But that was also what made him resolve to be the best caretaker for her that was possible. He had their fridge stocked with tons of drinks, smoothies, shakes, and yogurt; he had their cupboards filled with teas. Their bathroom was stocked with vitamins and their bedrooms had heating pads, fans, wet wipes, and a trash can specifically for if Clara couldn't make it to the bathroom.

Setting all of her things on the nightstand, he hurried to the bathroom and gave a knock. "Hey, I have all your stuff up here. Do you want some help to get back to bed?"

She let out a groan that sounded affirmative, so he opened the door to find her practically lying in front of the toilet.

"Oh Clara, that's no good."

"Floor is cool," was all she mumbled.

"I know, I know, but here, let me help you into bed where you can drink tea. Want me to put a cool washcloth on your forehead while you rest?"

She nodded and Nathan went about helping her to her feet. It wasn't exactly the easiest task. Clara was a whole lot of woman regularly, and now she was a whole lot of woman plus two. While Nathan loved the babies growing inside of her, while he was excited for them to come out and meet him, he couldn't mind if maybe they let up on their mother a little.

She was still beautiful to him, nothing could change that, but she looked peaked and drawn, her skin paper-pale with dark circles under her eyes almost like bruises. Her lips were chapped and cracked in the corners, while her normally well taken care of hair was a frizzy cloud around her head.

"Don't worry, I've got you."

Nathan took her hand, wrapping another arm around her waist, and slowly escorted her to their bedroom. He took as much time as she needed to get situated, still supporting her back as she sat down and sipped at the tea.

"Hey, if you want to sit up for a bit, would you like me to brush your hair?"

"Are you sure? It's a real mess. Greasy."

"I don't mind at all. You have that dry shampoo, don't cha? Want me to go grab that?"

She nodded gratefully and Nathan headed back to the bathroom, rooting around her toiletries basket until he found what he was looking for. Returning with her dry shampoo and two of the brushes he saw her use all the time, he slid into the bed behind her.

"Just relax, honey. I've got you."

Slowly, ever so slowly, he began his work. He started by spraying the very top of her head then slowly working his way down. He didn't know much about dry shampoo, but he knew he shouldn't use too much of it or it would make her hair look like there was baby powder. He also thought that he'd heard something about it needing time to absorb the oils as well, but he wasn't as certain about that.

There were plenty of snarls and tangles, but Nathan went through them methodically, working them down and out until there was just hair left. He traveled around Clara's head, checking in with her every so often.

"Thank you for doing this," she murmured when he was about halfway through.

"Of course. Whatever you need."

He knew that Clara wasn't feeling her best, to put it mildly, but he couldn't help but marvel at her. She was so powerful, carrying two full lives inside of her. Even though just waking up meant pain and suffering for her, he knew she didn't blame their kids. She had so much grace and optimism; Nathan knew he wouldn't be nearly as kind if he were in her situation.

But Clara was the best of the best, and she always encouraged him to be better than he was the day before. She was incredible, and if his girls turned out to be half the woman she was, well, he would be more than blessed.

Heart swelling in his chest from all the love and affection he felt for her, Nathan finished up her hair and started to braid it into a simple plait to keep it out of her face.

"Whatever you need, I'm here for you, okay?"

"I know," she murmured, turning to catch his cheek in a kiss. "I wouldn't be able to get through this without you."

His pride bubbled up at that, making his own cheeks flush. He didn't know what he'd done to have Clara trust him so implicitly, but he wasn't going to let her down. She was stuck with him, and he was going to take the best care of her, so they were together as long as possible.

He'd been given a second chance after being struck by lightning, and he wasn't about to waste it. No, he had a bright and happy future with the love of his life and their children, and he was more than ready to embrace it with open arms.

30

Charlie

The world was a small combination of dramatic things: the rest of it shut out to the back of Charlie's mind. There was the thundering of the bull's hooves. The dull roar of the audience. The harsh sound of his own breath rasping in his lungs as he ran.

It was borderline ritualistic, in a way. Like he was whisked away to a fantasy world with ancient challenges that only the most revered warriors were allowed to compete in. Maybe that was a little egotistical of him to think, but it was always fun.

Charlie vaulted over a hay bale, waving his arms to draw the attention of the bull away from the rider who was trying to escape. It worked, and it was his turn to run again.

A lot of people didn't know it, but there was a certain amount of skill that went with working as a clown for a rodeo. He had to know how to attract the bull, judge the best time to do it, and make sure that he always had a clear exit path. And that wasn't counting how he needed to keep track of all the other clowns around him, coming to the rescue whenever they were cornered, pinned, or just in a bad way.

"Come and get me!" he called, running to the next obstacle, a barrel that would be fairly easy to loop the bull around. It wasn't the most secure of boundaries, but it was close to the bull's gate so it should be easy enough for his trainer to beckon him into his cozy pen in the back.

Or at least that was what Charlie hoped. There always was a certain sort of unpredictability that came with working with live animals. At least the bull wasn't in pain like some other events he'd been to. The rodeo he worked with always treated the animals like royalty. Probably because bull riding was one of the most popular reasons that people cared to buy tickets.

He reached the barrel, turning on his heel again to put the bull in the right place, when suddenly something slammed into the side of his head. It knocked him off balance, and the next thing he knew, his ankle was twisting the wrong way and he slammed into one of the walls surrounding the pen.

The world spun, and Charlie blearily looked to what had hit him. And he couldn't believe it when his eyes landed on an unopened beer can on the ground beside him. Someone had chucked that at him? Sure, it wasn't unheard of. After all, patrons could get a little rowdy with a drink or two or ten inside of them. But the last time they'd had an issue with it had been at least a year or so ago.

Oh, right, there was a bull charging towards him.

Charlie tried to push himself up to his feet, fearing the worst, but that was when two of his colleagues jumped in front of him, hootin' and hollerin'.

"Hey now, why don't ya come follow me!?" The clown let out a whistle and clapped loudly before bolting away. Sure enough, it worked, leading the bull away and allowing two medics to come grab Charlie and haul him out.

That was how he ended up on one of the med cots in the back, the two flurrying over him as they checked for injuries.

"I'm fine, I'm fine," Charlie assured, trying to wave them off.

"You hit your head pretty hard out there. Let us do some safety checks."

They had a point. Charlie still felt a little lightheaded, his vision threatening to skitter this way or that. One of the medics shined a light in his eyes and he felt like he was about to barf.

"Whoa, chill there, friend."

"I'm pretty sure you have a concussion. We're gonna send you to the ER, alright?"

"Where is he? Is he okay?"

Daisy's sharp voice cut through the crowd. A moment later she was right in front of him, turning him this way and that.

"Babe, are you okay!?"

"Hey, yeah, I'm fine, but I won't be if you keep moving me around. Ow! Daisy, seriously, I'm fine!"

She let go of him but didn't look that relieved. "How is he? Tell me the truth?"

"We think he's got a twisted ankle and maybe a concussion."

"A concussion!?"

Charlie winced. "Hey, Daisy, I promise it's not too bad, but please, maybe not so loud."

"Sorry," she murmured, her face looking pinched. Charlie felt bad that he was stressing her out, but it wasn't like he intended to. "Did somebody really lob a beer into the ring?"

"Yeah," one of the other clowns said, ambling around a couple of the pens. Charlie guessed that the bull was contained then. "Security's already after him."

"I can't believe it! Don't they realize how dangerous that is? They could have shattered my husband's skull!"

"Thankfully, here I am, skull mercifully unshattered," Charlie tried to soothe. But Daisy wasn't having it. While she'd always been a passionate person, it was unusual to see her so rattled. "Come on. They're gonna send me to the ER to scan the old noggin. Let's get out to the parking lot so the ambulance can come pick me up."

"Hold on there, we'd rather you sit still for a while," one of the medics said, a calm hand on Charlie's shoulder.

"Really guys? You don't think you're being a *wee* bit paranoid?"

"Hey, listen to them. It's their job!" Daisy said, pulling Charlie into a hug. He did feel bad about worrying her, but it was in his nature to downplay things. After all, he was the Miller who kept his assault a secret for almost a quarter of his life. "You're not allowed to make me a widow or I'll march right to heaven where your soul's is hanging out and make you regret it!"

Hah, now that was certainly a picture. Charlie could see her marching right through the pearly gates, just to give Charlie an earful. She was his firecracker, that was for sure. Loyal, protective, and passionate even past the end.

"Don't worry. I'm not the abandoning type." He did sober a little at the thought, however. He knew how much losing his mother had stunted his father's life for years, leaving him lonely and in mourning. He would never, ever do that to Daisy if he could help it. He wanted a long and fulfilling life with her, no shortcuts. "Besides, I gotta stick around for our kids."

At that Daisy stiffened, and the curious reaction had Charlie pull away from her just enough to see her eyes widen while her face paled.

"How did you know about that!?"

"How did I know about wha—" Charlie's potentially concussed brain pulled up short and he put together the puzzle pieces that had just rapidly been dropped on him. "Wait a second." Daisy had been taking a lot more naps in the past couple of weeks. She'd also complained about craving red meat a lot. But other times she was nauseous.

"Are you *pregnant!?*" he blurted, forgetting that they were very much surrounded by people.

"I, uh... I mean..." Daisy took a steadying breath. "Um, surprise?"

"I was just kidding! I didn't know!"

"Well I didn't know you were kidding!"

A bunch of things flooded through Charlie's mind, one right after the other, but the most prevalent was joy. Pure, unadulterated joy. It nearly blinded him, making his head spin, but he still managed to pull Daisy to him in a hug.

"Why did you keep it a secret?"

"I was worried," she murmured, sounding so vulnerable and sweet against his neck. Thankfully, the two medics by him seemed to catch on that they were having a moment and backed away, allowing them a small modicum of privacy.

"Worried about what?"

"A lot of things."

"Like?"

If there was one thing that was a constant about their relationship, it was that they could tell each other anything. Worries, fears, mistakes, all of it.

"Losing it. My mother was told that she'd never have children because of her fibroids and a few other fertility issues. That's why I was an accident."

"Is that all?"

"I... I suppose I was worried about your reaction too."

Charlie couldn't blame her for that. They hadn't discussed having a baby at all, and that was normally something that did need a little conversation. He'd assumed it would be something they'd address in a couple of years or so, not in the first nine months of their marriage.

After all, it had taken him a long time to be able to be intimate at all. Lots of meetings with therapists and working through his fear their entire courtship. He'd wanted Daisy, because she was gorgeous, wonderful, and everything he wanted in a woman. But it took a lot of times of him saying 'no,' and her immediately listening to help him process a lot of the PTSD that was dominating so much of his life.

"I understand, honey, but I'm thrilled."

"You are?"

He nodded and tilted her head up so he could give her a gentle kiss. His head was still pounding, but it fell into the background noise of his mind. He was going to be a *father!*

"I love you, Daisy, and I couldn't be happier to start our family together."

She huffed the tiniest of laughs, then kissed him right back. "Me too."

"Whatever happens, we're in this together. You're stuck with me, through thick and thin."

"Through thick and thin," she repeated against his chest. Charlie held her, a bit scared, but more than ready for the next adventure in their life.

31

Daisy

aisy stared at herself in the bathroom mirror, feeling both numb and like she could drown at the same time. So much was happening in her mind; it was like a tempest surging in her skull. But at the same time, she felt like she couldn't come to grips with it, that she was living in some strange reality where only the worst happened.

But no, she was in real life, and the truth was that she was in the middle of a miscarriage.

It had started two days earlier with some pretty extreme cramps and nausea. Then it had been way too much blood in her underwear. She was just eleven weeks long, not even out of her first trimester, and it hadn't taken a genius to figure out that something was wrong. Charlie had whisked her away to the ER where the doctors there had confirmed the worst.

Her baby was no longer her baby, just a collection of non-living cells within her that her body was trying to pass. They'd given her the option to just let her body do what it wanted to on its own but explained that it could take weeks. Or she could use a thing called Misoprostol to help her body along.

Daisy had chosen the faster option. The thought of the whole thing dragging on made her feel sick to her stomach in the worst way. She wanted it over and done with, so she didn't have to be reminded of what was happening every time she went to the restroom.

Sure, she hadn't been sure if she'd been ready for a baby, and she remembered being terrified in the two weeks between her finding out and Charlie guessing the truth. But she'd gotten attached to the little bean growing within her. It felt like her joy, her dreams for the future had all been yanked away from her with little remorse.

Was it something she had done? Should she have been more careful? Daisy knew her mother had about four miscarriages before she had gotten her tubes tied, but Daisy had a hard time believing it was only that.

Was it her punishment for being a lush? She'd only fallen off the wagon once since she started dating Charlie, but what if this was punishment for that? Did she have her baby's blood on her hands? Or worse, what if her baby was taken away because she would be a terrible mother? What if being her progeny was literally a fate worse than death?

All of those churning thoughts made her want to sink into the floor, and Daisy found she was crying again. She felt like she hadn't stopped crying for three days, and goodness, she wanted a drink more than anything.

A knock sounded at the door, pulling her from her abysmal thoughts. "Daisy, you okay in there?"

"No," she answered honestly. Because while she may feel like she was going to break into a thousand heartbroken pieces, she didn't lie to her husband. Never to him.

"Can I come in?"

"Yeah."

The door slowly cracked open, and Charlie entered, a pill in one of his hands and her favorite jumbo-sized water bottle that only had to be put in a freezer for three hours and would keep her water cold all day long.

"You wanna go for a ride?"

"In your truck?" she asked, gratefully taking the medicine and swallowing it down. Although it was flavorless, it still tasted like the world's most bitter chalk to her. Like she was swallowing down her disappointment and hurt in physical form.

"No, on some horses. Maybe take a trot out to the new land we bought, mosey around the pond."

For a moment Daisy was going to refuse. She just wanted to hole up in their bed, bury herself under the covers and wallow in her grief. But the thought of sun on her face, a gentle wind on her back, and the company of her beloved was a lot more compelling.

"Yeah, I'd like that."

"Alright, why don't you take a nice, warm shower, then get dressed? I'll pack us some snacks for a kinda picnic or something."

"Thank you," Daisy said, her heart aching bittersweetly in her chest. The practical part of her knew that it was incredibly common for miscarriages in the first trimester, but the emotional side of her was so much louder.

"Of course," Charlie answered her, giving her a side hug and kissing the top of her head. "We're in this together. Through thick and thin."

"Through thick and thin," she repeated.

That little conversation was enough to get her to go through the motions at least, and after an indeterminate amount of time, she was ready to go riding. She met Charlie in the kitchen of the main house, then followed him out. She didn't say much, but she didn't need to. Charlie knew her better than she knew herself sometimes, and he got that she needed time to process.

Granted, there was an ever so tenuous line between processing and spiraling. Sometimes Daisy didn't know where that line was, so she was grateful to have him nearby.

"Hey, I was thinking maybe next month that we should go on a vacation."

"Vacation? Where were you thinking?" Daisy asked, surprised by the sudden non sequitur.

"You mentioned always wanting to go to Australia, right?"

"Close. New Zealand. I want to see where they filmed the Lord of the Rings." Daisy couldn't believe he remembered that. She loved Lord of the Rings, but she didn't mention it overly often. Usually because she was too busy talking about rodeo stuff.

"Yeah, let's go there. Maybe spend a couple of weeks just seeing whatever you want to and eating yourself silly."

The idea was certainly appealing, but when Daisy thought about bleeding on the plane, then bleeding as she wandered around the shire, the whole thing soured.

"Could we... could we maybe do next month? After this has all cleared up?"

"Of course," he answered, voice all soft and caring. Goodness, he was so wonderful. He made her feel like she wasn't being overly emotional or going off the deep end for mourning a baby that never really got to be a baby. "Whenever you're ready, just say the word. No rush."

Daisy nodded and returned to her contemplation as their mounts slowly walked along. She looked over the beautiful land that Charlie had purchased specifically for them to build their own house on. She couldn't believe how blessed she was that they had the wealth to do that. And that wasn't the end of their dreams. They were going to build some top-notch horse training facilities and actually get a good herd going. Not to mention an area for rescues. It was a dream come true, to be perfectly honest, and before three days ago, Daisy would have said she couldn't wait.

But now, after her entire world had shifted, she definitely could wait. In fact, she wished that the whole world would just pause for a second so she could feel everything she needed to feel and could act like a normal human again.

That wasn't how life worked, however, so she supposed she just had to keep clinging to life, keep processing everything she was going through.

Her gaze flicked over to Charlie, and she came to a sudden realization. Although she was certainly suffering, she wasn't the only one that had lost a child. Her husband had lost his baby too. And although he didn't have to physically handle the miscarriage, his heart still had to go through it.

"Can we have our picnic here?" she asked as they approached one of the few trees on their new land.

"You sure? You don't want to do it by the pond?"

Daisy shook her head, pulling her horse to a stop.

So Charlie did the same, helping her down, then beginning to set out everything their impromptu meal needed.

It was only a couple of minutes later when they were both sitting down on the large, comfy blanket with Daisy curled up against Charlie's side.

"I'm sorry you're going through all this," he murmured, gently stroking her hair as she settled her head into his lap. "But I'm here for you, okay? Anything you need, just ask. And I'll do my best to make sure that you don't even have to ask."

Daisy closed her eyes, willing herself not to cry. She just wanted a single hour without tears leaking down her face.

"What if we can never have kids, Charlie?"

He didn't say anything for a moment, his hand continuing to stroke through her hair. When he spoke, there was a heady sort of love in his tone. "Do you *want* to have children?"

Now it was Daisy's turn to pause and think about it. She'd always assumed that she'd never have a chance. She was so poor and so alone, falling into her bottle more often than not. But all of that had changed when she'd started dating Charlie.

He'd opened an entire world for her. They were best friends, lovers, and spouses. She was in it for the long haul with him, and everything that entailed.

"Yeah. I do. I want to have kids with you."

"Alright then. There's lots of options. We can try again, and if that doesn't work, we can look into fertility treatments. And if that doesn't take, we can look into other methods. Charity seems very happy with her son."

That was true. Jadyn was really flourishing, even after just seven months with his new family. Daisy loved seeing how much Charity glowed with the addition to her family, and she wouldn't be surprised if there were more kids in her future.

"And you'd be okay with that?" Daisy whispered, hardly daring to hope.

"As long as it's with you. Yes."

"What if I don't want to adopt?"

"Then we don't have to have a kid. I married to *you*, Daisy. I want a future with *you*. If that includes kids, then I'm all for it. But if it doesn't? That's okay too. I'll have plenty of nieces and nephews to dote on."

Daisy opened her eyes and looked up at the love of her life. She felt bolstered, a little less like she was going to topple over the edge of sanity.

"Thank you, Charlie. Really." Another deep breath. "I think... I think I would like to try again."

"Are you sure?"

"Yeah, maybe not now. But... after the holidays?"

He leaned down and pressed his lips ever so gently to hers. "I couldn't think of a better gift."

32

Cici

"Here comes the airplane!"

Cici made what she hoped was an engine sound as she made a spoonful of baby food wind through the air. Her niece, Persephone, let out a happy scream, then opened her mouth, allowing the mush to be deposited.

Naturally her twin, Penelope, was clearly offended that she wasn't the one getting the food and let out her own disgruntled sound. Cici rushed to get her a spoonful of her own, not wanting to cause a skirmish the very first time she was watching her nieces.

"You are an angel," Clara said from her bed where she was sipping tea.

Cici realized her sister had been through *so* much. Between her pregnancy's medical complications and having a C-section, she'd lost so much of her muscle and curves. She looked wane, drawn even. It was a wonder that her twins had turned out to be quite healthy sizes, nearly as big as single babies who got to gestate the full nine months.

But the important thing was that she was gaining weight bit by bit, and soon she would be able to do light labor. Cici knew that they'd all have to keep an eye on her anyway, because they all knew she tended to overdo things. But at least she'd have her babies to keep her distracted.

And goodness, were the pair a distraction.

Cici had seen babies before. Interacted with them. But she'd never fully been in charge of their care. Talk about jumping off the deep end by immediately babysitting twins.

"In for a penny, in for a pound," Cici murmured, filling another spoonful.

"What was that?" Clara asked.

"Oh, just thinking. Do you need any more tea?"

"No, I'm good on this for now."

"Have you had your ensure yet?"

Clara rolled her eyes, but her grin was loving. "Yes, *mother.*"

"And don't you forget it!" Cici said, sticking her tongue out.

Clara chuckled, but then winced. "Oof, if you could hold off on that brilliant sense of humor of yours, I would be much obliged."

"Sorry, I'll try to simmer down on my comedic brilliance."

"Thank you."

Clara settled further into her bed, nursing her tea while Cici finished up feeding the twins. After that, not much time passed before the room filled with a truly horrific smell.

"Ugh, what's that?"

"Smells like someone went potty. Do you need help with that?"

"Uh, yeah."

"Don't worry, the changing station I bought has wheels. Pull it over here and I'll show you how to put the brakes on, then what to do. That way you'll know what to do when you finally have your own."

"Have my own?"

Suddenly Cici's mind rushed off to what that would look like. Her chubby and full with child, her cheeks rosy and her skin glowing like Clara's had been before she'd gotten so ill. Maybe she'd finally inherit some of the curves her sisters had instead of being the slender one in the family.

And what would their babies look like? Would they have Baz's distinctive nose? His dark, thick hair? Would they have her eyes?

"Hey, you okay there?"

Cici blinked and returned to reality.

"Oh, yeah. I'm fine. You were saying?"

"You see that red pedal down at the bottom of the leg? Step on that to activate the brake. You must *always* have the brake on whenever a baby is on here, do you understand?"

Cici nodded adamantly and her sister went into a full demonstration on how to change a baby. To Cici, it was quite gross, with way more poop than a single baby should be able to produce, and there were *two* of them. No wonder Clara needed a little help.

"Alright, now it's your turn."

Swallowing hard. Cici tried her best, Clara helping her out through the second baby's diaper change until both were clean and happy.

"Goodness, they are cute when they're not making the whole room stink," Cici said, gently placing Penelope on Clara's lap while she took Persephone. "Do you know how cute you are, little Princess?"

"She's a queen, actually," Clara said primly. "And she certainly knows it."

As if she did indeed understand, the baby let out a knowing coo. Then her sister laughed and the two proceeded to babble at each other for a good four minutes.

Cici could definitely see the appeal. Sure, they were exhausting. And hard work. And occasionally stinky. But they were also bundles of joy with angelic faces and hilarious antics. She could hang around them forever, just listening to them be silly little, baby humans.

"Can you record this on your phone and send it to me?" Clara asked, looking like she could float up out of bed. "This is gold."

"Sure, can I place Persephone beside you?"

Clara nodded.

Cici did that, whipping her phone out as she backed up. The babies instantly reached for each other, their chubby fingers grabbing with all the dexterity one expected such freshly baked humans to have.

They laughed like they were doing a real comedy routine and Cici made sure to get it all on her phone. She was definitely going to send this to the rest of her family too.

Except maybe Charlie. It had been a few months since Daisy's early miscarriage, but Cici still got the impression that the topic was sensitive for them. Not that she could blame them.

She'd never really given much thought to babies. She and Baz had talked about it once maybe, and they'd both felt that they were far too young. Plus, watching Clara struggle with debilitating nausea had definitely discouraged Cici a lot. Who would want to willingly put themselves through something that made them vomit constantly, have their feet swell, their pelvis spread and a litany of other awful things?

But now that she was spending an entire day with the results of all that suffering... well, she could see how it might be worth it. Even when she left Clara's house utterly exhausted, Baz coming to pick her up in his hot rod, she wished that she could stay longer.

"Do you want me to come back tomorrow?"

"Oh no, that's alright. Papa and Jeanette will actually be dropping by, and I don't think I can handle much more company than that. I still get tired plenty fast."

"Okay, maybe this weekend then?"

Clara's grin was full of all that special kind of smarminess that only older sisters could have. "Why Cici, if I didn't know better, I would say that you might be taken with my baby girls."

"They're cute, okay? And it's not like we've gotten to spend much time together lately, with me taking over your chores on the ranch and you building up this homestead here."

"Cici, we have dinner together twice a week."

"Before you got real sick and even the smell of food made you double over in the bathroom."

"Ah... I suppose you're right. Funny how time is when you're out of it most of the time. But yes, this weekend is fine. Keep it up and I'm sure you'll be on your way to being their favorite aunt."

Cici huffed. "Man, Charlie has it so easy! He doesn't have any competition."

"Only until our cousins from up in Montana roll into town. I figure my kids will just call them all Aunt and Uncle. Feels less weird."

Cici nodded. While she knew it was perfectly normal for people to have cousins much older than them, it still didn't sit quite right with her. "Man, I don't envy these kids having to memorize all our names. We're basically our own platoon at this point."

"You're not kidding." Clara planted a kiss on Cici's cheek before retreating indoors. "This is about all I can stand before the pain sets in, so I'm going to go sink into my favorite recliner and have Nathan cook me dinner. See you this weekend, Cici."

"See you!"

Baz waved from the car as she approached, and Cici barely remembered to return it in a timely way. Her thoughts were too full of babies and growing a family. She was pretty sure that she'd just caught baby fever, but what was the point? Especially when Baz and her had already decided no, not now.

Ugh, it was such a bummer. But Cici forced herself to push the thoughts away and buckled up in the passenger's seat. She was sure that if she just distracted herself enough, the urge would go away.

33

Baz

Something was going on.

Baz didn't notice it right at first, but as the days ticked on, he started to notice a certain kind of crossness from his wife. Cici was almost always a bottle of effervescence and positivity, so while her actions weren't that egregious, they stood out.

And it wasn't just that she was being short with him. If she was, he'd assume that he'd somehow done something to upset her. But no, she was short with herself, and even upset with the movies and TV they would watch together after their dinners.

He knew that she was under a lot of stress with their house on the edge of town just being finished, but Cici didn't usually handle stress by being sharp with people. He knew her well enough to know that her go-to was withdrawing into herself and getting stuck in her own head.

"Ugh, be *careful*, Cici!" she said sternly to herself.

Her sharp tone drew Baz's attention and he looked over to see her running her hand under cool water, her coffee spilled all over the counter.

"Hey, are you okay?" he asked, hurrying over to her.

"Yeah, I'm *fine*, just being my normal, klutzy self."

Baz frowned. He didn't like when Cici put herself down, and he felt like it was happening more and more lately. Was something going on?

"Here, let me clean this up for you."

He hurried to wipe away the coffee and put more on for her, his mind ticking through anything that might be upsetting her. He knew her sister-in-law had a miscarriage a while back. And that Clara had been struggling with some sort of extreme morning sickness, but he thought most of that was sorted out by the time the twins had actually popped out.

"You don't have to. I was just being stupid."

Now that was enough. Setting his rag down, Baz looked to his beautiful but very clearly upset wife.

"What's wrong?"

"What do you mean, what's wrong? I spilled my coffee and burned my hand."

"No, I mean what's *really* wrong? You're being kinda mean to my best friend and I'm not a fan of it."

Her eyes widened and she looked at him in absolute shock. "Your best friend?"

"You, Cici. You're my best friend and you're being a real jerk to you." He didn't mention that she'd been gruff with him either. If she was already feeling bad, he didn't need to heap that guilt on top of everything.

"I..." She heaved a breath, her posture seeming to crumple. "I'm gonna sit down, okay?"

"Sure, you do that. I'll finish this up, then bring you a new cup. And you're sure your hand is okay?"

She nodded, her gaze already far away.

So clearly, he had been right. Something was bothering her. Part of Baz was proud that he could read his wife so well, but a very big part of him was worried about what could actually be upsetting her.

He cleaned up as quickly as he could, then hurried over to her, sitting beside her on the couch and taking her hand. Her face was cloudy, something he wasn't quite used to, and she still didn't say anything for quite a while.

But Baz waited for her to be ready. There was no point in rushing her when it was so very obvious that she was struggling with something.

"Do you remember how I babysat Clara's twins a couple of weeks ago?"

"Honey, you've been babysitting and helping your sister every three days or so for almost a month."

"Right. Yeah. Well, I guess you can say that I've become really attached to them."

"Well, that's great, right? They're your nieces, after all."

"I mean, yeah, it's a good thing, but there's also some unintended side effects."

That was certainly concerning. "Like what?"

"Like, uh, like I really want to have a baby now."

Baz stared for a moment. Then stared a little longer. "You what?"

"Look, I know it's not happening. And to be honest, I also

know I'm not ready. But there's this really consistent urge inside of me that just is *demanding* a baby.

"I know I'm too young, and after Charity's fertility problems, Clara's rough pregnancy, and Daisy's loss, I'm far too terrified to physically put myself through any of that. But this fight keeps going around and around in my head."

Baz hurried to catch up in the conversation, frustration clear in his wife's voice. He hated to hear her sound so conflicted. Cici had always been the determined type, deciding what to do and then doing it, so seeing her flustered was disconcerting.

"I'm mad at myself for being scared. I'm mad at myself for suddenly being baby obsessed. It's not like I'm endlessly maternal like Charity. She's basically been a mom since she was a teen with Mama passin'. I'm mad at myself for being too young. And I guess I'm kinda mad at the entire world for being so inconvenient."

"That's a lot to be mad about," Baz agreed. Huh, maybe he didn't have as much to be proud of with his husband senses because he'd had no idea that his wife was struggling so much. And with some heavy stuff too.

"You don't think I'm crazy for it?" she asked.

Baz shook his head, trying to tick through his thoughts quickly, but also carefully.

He hadn't thought about children much either. He and Cici had discussed it once around their honeymoon when they both decided it wasn't something they were interested in for the next three to five years. But he also didn't spend much time with Clara's babies—or anyone else's for that matter.

"No, I don't think you're crazy. But I understand why you might feel that way."

"What do I do? I obviously can't keep going this way. It's

making me miserable every single day. I keep telling myself to just get over it, but I can't. I literally can't bury these thoughts or even distract myself from them for longer than a few hours."

His poor wife. His poor, loving, empathetic, and wonderful wife. Baz tenderly took her hands into his own, looking deep into those Miller intense eyes of hers.

"Cici, if you want to have a baby that badly, I'm okay with trying."

"That's the thing. I'm *really* scared of all that. I don't want the stretch marks or the morning sickness, or a surgery where they have to cut my stomach open. It's *terrifying.* And I feel weak for thinking that when millions of women go through it all the time."

"You're not weak, Cecelia. We all have our fears, and those are all plenty legitimate."

"So what do I do then? I don't want to spend my entire pregnancy on edge. That doesn't sound like it would be very good for the baby."

His heart ached for her, it did. "What if you didn't have to have one physically?"

"What?"

"I think a big part of this is that you're very scared of the unknown. What if we made it a bit less unknown?"

"What do you mean?"

"Have you ever thought of fostering? The goal of it is the eventual reunification of children with their original families, or giving them a safe place to stay until adoption papers are able to go through the courts and all that.

"We could take care of a kid, learn a lot about parenting and if we're fit for it, and then decide where we go from there. It's different from the adoption your sister did, but still plenty important."

"How do you know so much about this?"

"Watched a couple documentaries about it when I had real bad insomnia before our wedding. That, and one about Peeps, then another about Nerf guns."

Cici looked at him like he'd just discovered daylight itself. "I... I would need to do some research, but yeah, that sounds like it could work."

Baz pulled her into his arms, holding her slighter frame against his. "I'll help you with whatever research you need. I'm here for you, Cici. I understand this isn't an easy or simple process, but I want to help you in whatever way I can."

"Thank you," she said, practically sinking into him. "I'm sorry that I've been so bitey lately. My mind has been, uh, cranky, for the lack of a better word."

"It's okay. But next time don't punish yourself so much. If you're feeling frustrated, you can talk to me."

"I'll try to remember that. I just felt so silly."

"You're not silly, Cici. Never." She gave him a look and he relented a little. "Okay, maybe you're a little silly when you tuck your hair under your nose like a mustache, but that's about it."

She laughed ever so slightly, leaning her head against his shoulder. "Thank you, Baz, really."

"No problem, my love. You've been there for me through some very dark times. The least I can do is listen and help out."

"It means a lot."

Baz hummed, holding her that much tighter. He didn't know if their future involved biological children, adoption, or fostering, but as long as Cici was in it, he was more than on board.

34

Jeanette

*J*eanette stirred the pot of mac n' cheese that she was cooking while Clara took a several-hour-long nap on the couch in the living room at the Miller house. She was twelve weeks out from her c-section and pretty much thoroughly healed, but she was still working on gaining a lot of the weight she had lost. She looked less like she was about to keel over any second, and her hands had stopped shaking every time she picked something up.

Naturally, she still needed way more sleep than she was getting, considering that she had twins, but Jeanette was happy to do her part to help with that.

"Besides, it's hardly work when I get to watch the two of you, is it?" Jeanette crooned to the portable crib she'd set up in the kitchen. That way she could watch the twins while she cooked and not have to worry about the baby monitor.

Granted, Papa had invested in a *very* fancy baby monitor, but sometimes it was nice to do things the old-fashioned way.

"It smells good in here."

A small voice caught Jeanette's attention and she turned to see Jadyn. He was a sweet but quiet little guy who didn't talk to her that often. Jeanette didn't take offense to it considering what he'd gone through, and she was sure that integrating into a new family of their size was pretty stressful on its own.

"Just making some mac n' cheese and corn dogs. Are you hungry?"

He nodded, pulling over a chair so he could sit right next to the crib. Jeanette watched without commentary, wondering what the young boy would do. For the most part, he just watched the dozing twins contentedly while she stirred more cheese and heavy cream into her noodles.

"So they're my cousins, right?" he asked finally, nearly startling Jeanette.

"Yes, they're your Auntie's babies."

More dutiful staring, as if he was trying to puzzle something out. "They're so big. I thought they'd be tiny."

"They were born a pretty good size, and they've been gaining weight like champions."

His brows furrowed and Jeanette swore she could hear the grinding of gears in his head. "I ain't been anyone's older cousin before."

"You haven't?"

He shook his head. "I didn't have much of anybody, really. Now I got all these people and new ones being born."

"Is it overwhelming?"

"What's that mean?"

"It means a lot. Like too much that makes it hard to think or feel good."

"Oooh, I get it. No, it's not overwhelming. But it's... more."

"More?"

The boy seemed to think for nearly a minute, Jeanette turning off the heat under her mac n' cheese. "More than I ever thought I would have. And everyone treats me like they're my real family."

"That's because they are."

"I know, and that's what's crazy. Peeps told me that I wouldn't really be a kid here, just a charity case. And people at school like to use that insult to make me mad. But that's not happening. Everyone talks to me like I'm a Miller."

"You *are* a Miller, Jadyn."

"I know. And I guess sometimes that's a little..."

"Overwhelming?"

He grinned at her. "Yeah."

Taking the corn dogs off the warming rack in the fancy deep fryer, Jeanette crossed over to the young man. He'd only been around a little under a year, but already he was such an integral part of their family. She certainly knew how much joy and fulfillment he'd brought Charity. She was meant to be a mother, through and through.

"Do you know the story of how I came to be here?" she asked.

He nodded yet again. "Mama Miller passed away like my gran when I was younger. He was really sad for a real, real, *real* long time until he met you."

"That's right. Then we fell in love and look where I am now! Would you say that I'm not a real Miller?"

"No. Everyone treats you like their Gran."

"Exactly. Me and you are in similar boats, you know? Meanies will try to take us down a peg by lying, but you and I know that we're loved. Really loved."

Jadyn grinned ever so slightly, giving one last nod before he was apparently done. "That food does smell awful good."

"Don't worry, I'll fix you a plate right up. You're a growing boy, aren't you?"

"Yes, ma'am!"

Chuckling, Jeanette set out to do just that. But as she grabbed a plate from the cupboard, she couldn't help but feel so incredibly blessed. She'd spent so much of her life utterly alone, and she'd assumed that was just her lot in life.

Clearly that wasn't the case. She had children and even grandchildren, a whole loving family for her to love and grow with. Emphasis on the growing, because she was pretty sure Charity was thinking of adopting again since it was such a long process, and Cici had been staring at the twins awful hard lately.

Yes, her life had certainly changed for the better since meeting the Millers, and she couldn't wait to see what happened next.

35

Papa

*P*apa Miller sat on his porch swing, sipping at peach tea while his whole brood had a cookout in the front. It wasn't a special holiday or anything, but when Cassidy had gotten a hankering for some grilled pork chops and Clara mentioned the doctor telling her she needed to eat more red meat and broccoli for the iron, it had all snowballed into having a real shindig.

Not that Papa minded, not at all. Charity, Mick, and Clara were all beasts at the grill, so much so that he wasn't really needed like he would have been ten years ago. Although Clara was sitting this one out, dozing on and off next to him on the porch swing. Poor girl, she was still recovering in a lot of ways. Papa loved seeing her so happy with her baby girls, and he approved of how Nathan doted on her, but watching his girl go through so much pain and anguish had been pretty awful. He remembered waking up multiple times, being afraid that he'd get a call about her pregnancy taking a turn for the worse.

But she was happy and almost healthy, and that was what mattered to him.

"Would you like some more tea, my love?" Jeanette asked, popping her head out from the front door.

"No, still working on this one," Papa replied.

"Alright. I'm just finishing up with the punch, then I'll be right out."

"Whenever you want, dear."

She nodded and ducked back inside, leaving Papa to look out at the goings-on. Everywhere his eyes landed were smiles and adoring expressions, filling his heart with warmth. From the twins, to Jadyn, to Nathan even, everyone looked to be having a great time. They really were a family, one cohesive unit.

And if Papa thought about it, even their relationships with their extended families were doing better. McLintoc had sent a holiday card and some of his sons and their partners visited in the past year. They had a big family reunion scheduled where everyone was pretty much set to attend, set in a middle location instead of just at the Montana Miller's.

He really was blessed.

"I wish you could see this, Mama," he murmured, knowing that no one was around to hear him. "You'd be right happy at how everyone is doing."

He knew she would, without a doubt. He could still remember the soft smile she'd have whenever she was particularly pleased, and the way her eyes would get misty whenever she was proud of their kids.

But unlike before, now he could think of her with only appreciation and love. There was no more guilt, no more toxic, thick negativity that made him want to shrink in on himself. He could love Mama but still keep room in his heart for Jeanette.

And she wasn't some sort of consolation prize. No, Jeanette was wonderful all on her own and he was blessed, oh so blessed, that their paths had crossed. Every day he said a prayer of gratitude for that, and that he was able to finally listen to his kids long enough to actually romance her.

"Got my punch," Jeanette said, sliding in the gap between him and Clara. "Goodness, it smells so good already."

"That's Charity. She makes amazing fiesta lime chicken breasts."

Jeanette nodded. "I remember I had those last fourth of July. Funny, for Clara and you dominating in the kitchen, all your kids seem to know how to cook at least a couple meals."

"Yeah, I made sure that all of them had the necessary skills to provide for themselves. Clara just took to it like a duck to water."

"I'll say. I hear that's how she tamed Nathan over there."

"Her roasts probably had something to do with it." Papa chuckled and drew Jeanette into his arms, ever so grateful for her. "By the way, have I told you I love you lately?"

"Nearly every morning, but I don't mind you saying it again."

"Good, cause I love ya."

"I love you too, Montgomery Miller."

Papa glowed at that, giving her a good squeeze. Maybe some would think that was cheesy or forced of them, but that was fine. Papa didn't love for the approval from other people. He loved with his full heart, knowing that time was never, ever promised.

Looking around again, he took in the wonder of everything that was around him. His laughing kids, his *grandkids*, the happy animals and expanded garden. And as the sun just began to set, its golden rays sinking into the dark velvet embrace of night, Papa realized he was truly content. After decades of loneliness, he finally had it all.

And he was never going to take that for granted.

HELLO READER! If you're reading this, you've probably read through all of the beloved Miller family stories. I hope you loved getting know everyone.

If you're ready for more, I've got another wonderful contemporary western world too! Copper Creek. This series has had several Kindle All-Star bonuses over the past few years, so readers are loving it. As of January 2024, I've written two complete interconnected series and am on the third one now. The first two series are B*aker Brothers of Copper Creek* and *Callahans of Copper Creek*. The third that I'm currently working on is titled *Keagans of Copper Creek*.

YOU CAN FIND the *Copper Creek Romances* on Amazon, but soon they will likely be on sale at my storefront too. I'll be sure to let you know when! Thank you for being a loyal reader.

Made in the USA
Columbia, SC
26 October 2024

44756425R00155